Clues to the Excitement about
Three-time Edgar Award Nominee
ROBERT BARNARD

"Barnard is an amusing Englishman with an eye for the self-delusion and hypocrisy in all of us . . . and the result is a growing series of mysteries that are entertaining . . . quite funny . . . and acutely observing."
—*The Boston Globe*

"There's no one quite like Robert Barnard in his ability to combine chills and chuckles and then sprinkle the whole with delicious irony."
—*The San Diego Union*

"If P. D. James is the heir to Dorothy Sayers, Robert Barnard is fast taking on the Christie/Marsh mantle . . . the most appealing and reliable practitioner of the classic British mystery to arrive here in the last decade."
—*Kirkus Reviews*

"One of the funniest new writers to emerge."
—*Ellery Queen's Mystery Magazine*

By the same author:

OUT OF THE BLACKOUT
CORPSE IN A GILDED CAGE
SCHOOL FOR MURDER
THE CASE OF THE MISSING BRONTË
A LITTLE LOCAL MURDER
DEATH AND THE PRINCESS
DEATH BY SHEER TORTURE
DEATH IN A COLD CLIMATE
DEATH OF A PERFECT MOTHER
DEATH OF A LITERARY WIDOW
DEATH OF A MYSTERY WRITER
DEATH ON THE HIGH C's

QUANTITY SALES

INDIVIDUAL SALES

Fête Fatale

ROBERT BARNARD

A DELL BOOK

Published by
Dell Publishing Co., Inc.
1 Dag Hammarskjold Plaza
New York, New York 10017

This work was first published in Great Britain as *Disposal of the Living*.

Dell ® TM 681510, Dell Publishing Co., Inc.

ISBN: 0-440-12652-5

Reprinted by arrangement with Charles Scribner's Sons

Printed in the United States of America

March 1987

10 9 8 7 6 5 4 3 2 1

WFH

CONTENTS

1   Hexton-on-Weir   7
2   Christian Spirit   16
3   Father Battersby   26
4   Battle Lines   41
5   Watery Bier   51
6   Curtains   68
7   Cold Steel   76
8   Our Gallant Boys   88
9   Castle Walls   97
10   Chez Mipchin   107
11   Thyrza at the Vicarage   116
12   Secrets   122
13   Delusions of Grandeur   131
14   At Li Chen's   143
15   The Westons   152
16   Seeing the Light   162
17   Final Accounts   167
18   Afterwards   180

NOTE

Yorkshire buffs will recognise that certain architectural features of Hexton-on-Weir in this book are taken from a well-known Yorkshire town. All the more necessary, then, to insist that the general characteristics of Hexton are my own invention, and that all the characters are totally imaginary.

Fête Fatale

CHAPTER 1

HEXTON-ON-WEIR

In the first place, Hexton-on-Weir is in possession of the Amazons. That you have to remember throughout this story. I noticed it days after I moved to the town, newly married, and I said so to Marcus.

'It's the women who rule in Hexton,' I said.

'Nonsense,' said Marcus. 'You just think that because you're a vet's wife, and women are always bringing their animals in. There's hardly a woman on the town council.'

'I'm not talking about town councils. I'm talking about the—I don't know—the *tone* of the place; the ethos. The voices that you hear are women's.'

That was it, really. It was something the casual visitor might not notice, or not in the first hour or two. There are men walking the streets, and shops that cater for the needs of men: tobacconists that still specialize in pipes, rather tweedy gentlemen's outfitters, and sporting shops where one could buy the wherewithal to deal death to fish and fowl.

But when you'd been in the town for a bit—and by the time this story opens I had been there for twelve years or so—you realized that the dominant tones that you heard were female. It was a woman laying down the law to a shopkeeper, a woman who was haranguing a police constable in the square about dog shit on the pavements, a woman who was exchanging heavy pleasantries with the tea-shop proprietor. And these dominant tones were a sort of middle-class lingua franca, with only occasional notes of Yorkshire (in which Hexton-on-Weir is very centrally embedded).

Gradually, in the early years of my marriage, I began to appreciate the standing of the men. However solid they might be physically, they had the status of appendages: they carried, they followed, they agreed. Their voice was low, their tone was mild—rather like the Victorian maiden's. Legally they were all the householder, but they did not aspire to be head of the house. When they retired here—and Hexton was very much a place to which people came to die, though many took a long time over it—some of them wilted in the overpoweringly feminine atmosphere. But others flourished in an environment where the troublesome business of decision-making had been taken off their shoulders: they adopted traditional roles such as the gay old dog, the father-confessor to the younger generation, the 'bit of a wag'. But, in essence, they were marginal, and they knew it.

Marcus came round to acknowledging this a couple of years after we were married.

'You were right, of course,' he said. 'The town council has nothing to do with it. Hexton is run by the women.'

Marcus was in a position to know. He had served briefly on the town council, as an Independent (that is, an old-fashioned sort of Tory-with-a-conscience), and he was a churchwarden who gave a great deal of his spare time to church matters. I stood for the council a year or two ago, for the Alliance, but I did not get in: none of the women voted for me, or allowed their husbands to.

It was Marcus in his role of churchwarden who made the remark that—rightly or wrongly—I always think of as the beginning of the trouble.

'You'll call on Mary, won't you, Helen?' he said, one evening in early April, he as usual sitting solid and comfortable in his chair by the fire, surrounded by a veritable whirlpool of pipe-smoke. Marcus was big, solid and unflappable, and always liked to do the right thing.

'Oh God—do I have to? It's not as though the old lady's

death was unexpected. Or particularly regrettable, come to that.'

'Mary's bound to miss her, after nursing her all these years. And since we have no vicar at the moment—'

'I *will* call on Mary, since it's the done thing in Hexton, but I'm damned if I'm going to act as surrogate vicar's wife,' I said, with some spirit.

'Good girl,' said Marcus comfortably. 'Give her my condolences, won't you?'

So there I was, committed to a visit of condolence to Mary Morse—one of those old-fashioned conventions of Hexton that I often enjoyed flouting and never enjoyed following. Old Mrs Morse had once been a powerful force in the town: a grim-looking, starchy, disapproving presence. In the last few years she had lost much of her position as a touchstone of respectable conduct and had become, in fact, quite childish. Her death, you might say, had been coming on for some time, but of course I made all the right noises when I went to pay my call on Mary.

'*So* good of you to come,' said Mary for the second time, pouring from the best teapot into the best teacups. 'One values one's friends at such a time.'

So little did I count myself her friend that as I settled back in my chair with my cup I could not remember when I had last been in that room. The curtains were drawn, but no extra light had been put on, so I had to peer rather to make out the contours of the furniture. It was old but good, in a standard sort of way, and it was kept immaculately polished. I have always thought that if there is one thing that I would rather die than hear said about me, it is 'she keeps her house spotless'. But it was said of Mary, and she smiled in quiet self-satisfaction if she heard it said. On the sideboard there were pictures of the Morse boys—men, rather. There had been two sons, but they had both left Hexton-on-Weir, as young men did tend to: they scuttled away from the overpoweringly feminine (or rather female) atmosphere. One of the Morse boys had scuttled to Australia, and wrote at Christmas. The other had gone to Scunthorpe, and was never mentioned—whether because he had gone to the bad, or because Scunthorpe was not the sort of place either Mary or her mother cared to mention, I had never found out.

'One misses Mother so much,' Mary was saying. 'But life must go on, of course.'

'Quite,' I said briskly, peering at my little triangle of sandwich in a vain attempt to find out what I was eating. 'Do you think of taking a job?'

'A job?' said Mary, with a hint of outrage in her voice. 'Charity work, do you mean?'

'Actually I meant a paid job—now you no longer have to nurse your mother. I'm sure there are lots of things that you could do.'

'Possibly,' said Mary, pursing her lips primly. 'Fortunately I have no need to take paid employment. I shall be comfortably off. Mother saw to that. I'm sure Mother wouldn't at all have liked the idea of my taking a *job*.'

'I thought it would give you an interest,' I said, ignoring her obvious displeasure, as I always did when I had decided that I really could not restrict my conversation to the sort of things that Hexton wants to hear. 'Fill in the time.'

Mary glared at me, prim-lipped, her hands linked in the lap of her drab grey woollen dress—a dress that was quintessentially Hexton. The tone of her voice was designed to stamp on this topic of conversation once and for all.

'I'm very far from needing things to fill in my time. With the house, and the garden, and so many interests in the town. You're still a newcomer really, Helen dear, so you probably hardly remember how *active* I was before Mother's sad illness. In fact, there was something I wanted to have a word with you about—do *please* have another sandwich, my dear.'

I took another little triangle. Cream cheese, I had decided, and as near tasteless as made no difference. I waited with foreboding for Mary's 'word'.

'Of course this really isn't the time, but perhaps since you're here I ought to seize the opportunity, and so far as I can judge the matter is *urgent*. It's about the new vicar—'

I swallowed the tip of the triangle and resumed my briskest manner.

'As far as *that's* concerned, you'll have to talk to Marcus. As you know, I'm a mere Sunday attender. If it wasn't for Marcus, I don't suppose I'd be that.'

'Quite, my dear. We all know that. What I'm hoping for is your influence *as a wife*.'

And there, of course, was the rub. The influence, the dominance, of the women of Hexton had not been achieved under the inspiration of any vulgar, modern feminist notions. Indeed, should any notable feminist have had the temerity to show her face in Hexton, she would most likely have been lynched in the genteelest possible way. In Hexton one used the time-honoured devices by which women have achieved power—not, of course, the devices of the courtesan, but those of the wife: the curtain lecture, the non-stop domestic needling. Mary did not see the fact that my husband was a devout and involved Christian whereas I was barely a believer as any bar to my exercising these traditional and successful Hexton levers of power. In fact, our marriage was not at all of the Hexton type, but if I had said to Mary that Marcus and I discussed things and then went our own ways, she would simply have refused to understand me.

'I think Marcus is much more likely to agree with *you* on church matters than he is with me,' I said, taking another sandwich. Watercress, of all the loathsome fillings. 'I'm not at all sure that you and I are likely to take the same point of view.'

'Oh, *this* is something you could hardly disagree about,' said Mary triumphantly, as if even my cussedness had its limits, 'My dear, I've heard a whisper that the Bishop intends to give the living to Battersby—Battersby of St Bride's, in Sheffield.'

'Oh,' I said blankly. Mary was looking at me so knowingly that after a minute I had to add: 'I'm afraid I'm not really up in clergymen—unless their sex lives get them into the *Yorkshire Evening Post*. What exactly is wrong with Mr Battersby?'

'*Father* Battersby he calls himself. And that's my point, my dear: he is quite incredibly *high*.'

'Well, it makes a change.' I knew at once I'd said the wrong thing, and was delighted. I went on, out of sheer malice: 'The Reverend Primp was an old dear in many ways, but you can't say he brought much colour and drama to the services, can you?'

'I don't think you'll find that people in Hexton want *that* kind of change. Colour and drama? This is religion! We've always had a very traditional and unexceptionable kind of service here. Nothing extreme. Not *too* evangelical, of course, but none of the more *showy* kinds of ritual either. Leave that to the Romans, as Mother used to say. We have our own ways. But Helen, dear, I don't think you are understanding the real *crux* of the problem.'

'No doubt I'm not,' I said. 'I'm very stupid on church matters.'

Mary leaned forward dramatically.

'The fact is, Father Battersby is a *celibate*.'

She hissed it, very much as she might if she were accusing him of pederasty or leather-fetishism. I refrained from saying that so far as I knew her own life had not in its first forty-five or so years been marked by unremitting copulation.

'Well,' I said, 'that's hardly a matter that it would be easy to use as an objection.'

'It most certainly is!' said Mary. 'Father Battersby is not just a bachelor, which would be bad enough: he is a celibate on principle. So that, though he is quite a young man, there is no question of there ever being a vicar's wife. Think of it!

A celibate vicar is quite inconceivable here in Hexton. The parish revolves around the vicar's wife. What would Mr Primp have been without Thyrza? Nothing! Less than nothing! I can't imagine what the Bishop is thinking of. He has the disposal of the living.'

I shivered presciently. 'What an unpleasant phrase.'

'It simply means that the decision is his alone. But he should take account of the congregation's wishes. Has nobody made him aware of them?'

'That would be Colonel Weston's job,' I said hurriedly. 'He's the senior churchwarden.'

'Quite. And one can only conclude that Colonel Weston has *not* been doing his job. That's why I do so want you to have a word with Marcus.'

'Well, I'll certainly tell him how you feel about it,' I said dubiously. 'I really have no idea of his views on the subject. I know he'll want to hear your views, if he knows you're worried.'

'Not just *me*, dear. Please don't give him the idea that I'm being selfish or quirky about this. It's the whole parish who will object if the Bishop does dispose of us in such an unsuitable way. And *please*, Helen *dear*, *do* emphasize to Marcus that I've nothing personal against the *man*. Your husband is so good-natured—I'd hate him to think there was any feeling against Father Battersby *himself*. As a person.'

'It's just his ritual and his wifelessness that's the problem. Yes, I'll make sure Marcus understands that.'

Mary gave me a long, cold stare.

'From your tone, Helen, I rather gather that you're not taking this altogether seriously. Of course I know you're not a church person by birth, but I do think you might try to enter into Marcus's interests more thoroughly. I assure you, it's not something I'm taking up in any light spirit. I feel it *deeply*. I think I owe it to Mother's memory to do something about it.'

I sighed. If that was to be the line of argument, there was

no opposing or ridiculing it. The matter of the new vicar
had been declared a sacred cause by the spirit of the late
Mrs Morse, the Blessed Gertrude. I saw through the dim
gloom the grim set of Mary's thin lips. Mary, without a
doubt, was to be the subject's leader and orchestrator, the
protector of Middle Church against the inroads of Popery.
It was a role that Mrs Morse had often played in the past,
for there was nothing ecumenical about her sort of Christian
spirit, and now by some kind of apostolic succession it had
descended on Mary. Even in her mother's lifetime, Mary
had been no mean concerter of outrage. She it was who had
spotted Hexton's first male ear-ring, she who had scotched
the idea of bingo in the church hall, she who had had the
trading licence revoked of the town's first and last video
library. Now, it seemed, she was moving by natural pro-
gression to the central position she had always aspired to.

'I'll talk to Marcus about it,' I said, feeling that I had
done all that convention demanded, and getting to my feet.
'Though of course, as you know, it's Colonel Weston who
is the senior of the two churchwardens.'

'Naturally I've spoken to Mrs Weston, but what can a
wife do if her husband has no backbone? In my experience
there is nothing so weak as a military man. I expect the
Bishop rode roughshod over such protests as he saw fit to
make.'

'Well, if Colonel Weston has already been—' I was about
to say 'got at', but I drew back—'approached, I don't
suppose you will do much good with Marcus. He would
never go behind the Colonel's back.'

'It may be necessary to go behind the Colonel's back,' said
Mary forcefully. We were at the sitting-room door, and she
suddenly changed her tone. 'Oh, Helen—I've just remembered that I wanted to talk to Marcus about Sophronia.'

Mary's manœuvre was quite transparent: she saw that I
was likely to be a lukewarm advocate, and she wanted to
put her case herself. I looked at the easy chair where

Sophronia Tibbles, a lazy and evil-minded Persian, dozed oblivious, dreaming dreams of the slow dismembering of mice.

'She looks healthy enough.'

'She's bringing up so much. I think maybe she's missing Mother. Of course normally I'd bring her to Marcus's surgery . . .'

'All right,' I said, suppressing a sigh. 'I'll tell him to call.' And I'll tell him there's nothing wrong with your damned cat too, I thought.

As we crossed the hall, Mary took up a couple of library books from the hall stand.

'Oh, Helen, I wonder if you would be so kind as to return these two to the library? At the moment, of course . . .'

I felt I learned more and more about the minutiæ of Hexton *mores* every day that I lived there. Now, after twelve years, I was discovering that it was not permitted to take your cat to the vet or to change your library book during the first fortnight of mourning. Was there some point, I wondered, some intermediate state of half-mourning, during which it was permitted to take your cat to the vet, but not to change your library books? It was no wonder, with a code of such subtlety, that I was stepping on toes from morning to night. I took the books from her and looked at them.

'Oh, Barbara Pym, how nice. So restful, with all that church activity,' I said, with sardonic intent.

'She's just a little too *modern* for me,' said Mary. 'So little of what I'd call story, don't you feel? I can't see her ever replacing Angela Thirkell.'

'She certainly won't *now*,' I said. 'But I'm sure there's a waiting list at the library. And for the C. P. Snow, now that he's on television.' Mary had opened the front door a fraction, and I blinked as the murk was pierced by a shaft of sunlight. 'Oh, splendid. The sun has come out.'

Mary was peering through a crack in the door.

'Oh dear—*look* at Roote. How vexatious. He has no *idea*

of how to prune. Men simply shouldn't be allowed to do it —they're nowhere *near* ruthless enough. Will you tell him as you go by, Helen: cut *closer*. Tell him he won't do any good by being so timid.'

It was typical of Mary, and typically aggravating, that she should have a gardener called Roote, that she should pay him less and get more work out of him than any of the rest of us in Hexton, and that she wasn't even pleasant to him.

'I suppose I can try, though I don't think Roote will want me telling him his business . . . Well, goodbye, Mary. I'm glad you're getting over things, and beginning to take an interest. I do hope you will come round and have a little supper with us when—' I wanted to say 'when the statutory period of court mourning is over', but I concluded lamely: 'when things have sorted themselves out for you.'

'I shall love to. Of course at the moment I'm still feeling Mother's loss . . . *terri*bly.' She dabbed at her eyes. 'But I mustn't forget that in the future I shall be freer, freer to do more. And freer to take an interest in the town. Mother's going was a release for her, but in a way it was one for me too. Now that she's gone, I can really be myself.'

Contemplating the new Mary as I walked down the driveway, I wondered whether that was really such a good idea.

CHAPTER 2

CHRISTIAN SPIRIT

It was brought home to me in the following few days just how little Mary's ability to organize outrage was impaired by the exigencies of Hexton's mourning customs. It was the week before Easter, and perhaps that put religion into people's minds, though really the spirit in which they went about it seemed more akin to the people who cried 'Crucify him!' than to anything I would care to call Christian. In the places where people met in Hexton they appeared to be talking of little else, and with a relish for the fray that seemed to recall the days of bare-fisted prize-fighting.

Hexton-on-Weir is a town of stone houses, most of them very old and slightly cramped, centred around a town square which is not a square, but a highly irregular form unknown to geometry. In the centre of this square is a church, a fine building which has fallen into disuse as a place of worship, and has been turned into a museum to a famous regiment whose barracks are a few miles out of town. The present parish church is now a smaller one, in a hollow to the east of the town centre. The other most notable architectural feature of the town is the castle, situated on a promontory, surrounded by a path, and overlooking a steep descent to the river and the weir. The castle probably had some military purpose at the time it was built, but if so it has never served it. Its only brief importance in seven hundred years was when Mary of Scots bed-and-breakfasted there during her English imprisonment. From the path around the castle, a favourite with dog-walkers and, in the evenings, with court-ing couples, one can see the meadows, where many sporting events take place, and where various social and horticultural functions are held in the summer months. For the rest, the old part of the town meanders up and down hill, in streets that are called 'wynds'— thigh-torturing streets they are, too, to the tourists who are not used to them, though they seem to produce in the residents a certain hardiness which no doubt contributes to their longevity.

The classes mingle, in Hexton, but in an aware, slightly prickly way, such as used to be common, my parents told me, in wartime. Hexton is, in its modest way, an anachronism, which the modern world intrudes on cautiously. Tourists come in summer, but as they rarely stay longer than overnight they make only a passing impact. The barracks, eight miles away, sends its high-spirited, loud-voiced youth into town at weekends, to drink, play billiards, and chat up such local girls as there are. My husband once told me that in the gents' loo in the centre are scrawled various suggestions as to how 'lads' can earn £5 to £10 in a simple and unde-manding way; but whether they ever take advantage of these offers—and who makes them—I have no idea. In general, Hexton takes the military in its stride, though it grumbles and calls them names; and at moments of national crisis, such as the Falklands affair, they readily cover them with a halo of patriotic warmth, and talk about 'our gallant boys', where previously they had been 'those hooligans'.

Similarly with racial minorities. Black or brown faces were seldom to be seen in Hexton, but many of the corner shops on the outskirts were owned and run by Indians or Uganda Asians, and 'men of colour' also ran one or two of the restaurants and take-away food places, as well as the splendid delicatessen on the square. These immigrants were all so quiet and obliging, and were so respectful in their demeanour, that they were unhesitatingly voted an asset to the town, and gave the middle-class residents a quite de-licious sense of après-Raj.

It was in the delicatessen owned and superbly run by Mr Ahmed Hussein that I first realized the extent of the trouble that Mary Morse was brewing up. Hexton is full of off-licences and undertakers, but Mr Hussein's is the only delicatessen, and he is generally found to be quite indispens-able—especially at such a time as Easter, when modest entertainments are planned, and something a little special is called for. As usual, Mr Hussein stood behind his refriger-ated counter, beaming over the cheeses, the pâtés and the salami at Mrs Nielson, a widow recently arrived in Hexton; while in the self-service part of the shop stood Mrs Franchita Culpepper with her Rottweiler puppy Oscar, brought in in blithe disregard of the 'No dogs PLEASE' notice on the door.

Oscar was built like a tank, but gazed out on the world with eager amiability, ever ready to wag his rump and the stump of his tail. Mrs Culpepper could also, as she surged through town, put one in mind of a tank—but in her case a more aggressive variety, for she usually showed a ferocious eagerness for the fray—any fray.

'I hear Mary's going to nobble your Marcus,' she brayed at me, baring her splendid array of teeth as she waded straight in, as was her wont. 'And quite right too. Never heard such a silly proposal. The congregation simply won't stand for it.'

Mrs Culpepper was to my certain knowledge an Easter communicant and not much more at St Edward the Confessor's, our parish church. But though I had a sneaking fondness for her, I also had the general awe, and I did not remind her of this.

'I must say I can't work up any great enthusiasm for the cause,' I said.

'*That* I heard, too,' boomed Franchita. 'You're wrong, you know. I wouldn't trust one of those celibate clergymen an inch. First thing you know, he'll be arrested for feeling up a plain-clothes policeman in a Soho club. Or he'll want to do a drag act at the church social. No, no: it just won't do at all.'

'Aren't you rather prejudging the poor man?'

'Not at all. Once upon a time gentlemen used to go into the church, if they hadn't any money and couldn't do any better for themselves. Not any more. There are so many weird types getting ordained these days that you've got to be damned careful if you're going to get one who's half-way sane. If it's not sex, it's nuclear disarmament or poverty in the Third World. What we want here is a good, safe, sane, middle-of-the-road man, with a nice, dowdy wife who wears hats.'

She looked around in irritation at the counter, where Mr Hussein was patiently holding out his hand.

'No, Mrs Nielson, three pounds forty. Here is only three twenty. That's right now. Who is next, please?'

'Me,' bellowed Franchita. 'Howard—how much are the tinned mussels?' I had not realized till then that, lurking in the shadows in the corner, was Howard Culpepper. 'Seventy-five? No—put them back. They're cheaper at Goodfayre. Right now, Mr Hussein, I'll just have four ounces of the Bel Paese. Oh, Oscar, *naughties*!'

Oscar, bored, had bopped down in the middle of the linoleum floor and let forth a stream of primrose liquid.

'Oh, Mr Hussein, do you think Mrs Hussein could—? Splendid! How much is the Bel Paese? Sixty-three? Christ, what a price! Well, here you are. Come along, Howard!'

And Franchita Culpepper charged out of the shop, leaving behind sixty-three pence and a pool of dog pee. Mr Hussein's smile gained a certain accretion of steel: thus must the merchants of Pankot have smiled at the English memsahibs at the approach of Independence Day, nineteen forty-seven.

A flustered-looking Mrs Nielson had retreated from the counter, and had accosted me. She was a once-handsome woman in her fifties, who also ignored the notice about dogs, but at least had the grace to carry her poodle, Gustave, in her arms. We gazed at the firm set of Franchita's shoulders as she departed, followed by Oscar on an actual lead and Howard on a symbolic one.

'Oh dear,' said Mrs Nielson, 'Mrs Culpepper does seem to be spoiling for a fight.'

'She always sounds like that, even if she's just complaining that the wrong newspaper's been pushed through her door,' I explained. And I added, because I thought it was true: 'It's mostly noise. She's not an ill-natured woman.'

'Oh, I'm sure ... I wasn't suggesting ... I'm so new here, I don't really catch the *nuances*,' explained Mrs Nielson.

'Mrs Culpepper keeps a hat shop and a husband,' I informed her. 'The hatshop doesn't make any money, I don't suppose, but it gives her an interest. We all buy hats there now and then, probably because we think that Franchita with an interest is a lot more bearable than she would be without one. Hexton-on-Weir must be one of the few places left that can support a hat shop. There are certain occasions when a hat is *de rigueur* here.'

'And the husband?'

'I believe he was retired early from a university some-where or other. I think they simply stopped doing whatever it was he taught. He says "Yes" and "No" very prettily, and that's about all I know about him. He has a pension, and she has a bit of private money, so they manage quite nicely. But her enthusiasm in this new vicar business is quite spurious. She hardly ever comes to church—and *never* in the winter, which according to Marcus is the real test.'

'I'm only an occasional attender myself,' Mrs Nielson said, and added in a rush of confession: 'More to get to know people than anything else. That's rather terrible, isn't it— *using* religion like that. Actually, I happened to be there for the last sermon of the previous priest—the Reverend Primp, wasn't that his name? I suppose it wasn't a fair test, he being so close to his heart attack, but he wasn't very exciting.'

'He never was. Dull as ditchwater. That's what they want here: someone who'll confirm all their existing ideas. An exciting man would never fit in, not in Hexton. Perhaps that's what they're afraid of with Father Battersby. Maybe they think his celibacy would make him exciting.'

By now Mrs Hussein had brought a newspaper and a bucket and cloth, and evidence of Oscar's visit had been removed. I went up to the counter to make my purchases, and I put the matter out of my mind.

Nobody else did, though. I was aware, wherever I went during that week, that nobody was talking about anything else. Buzz-buzz it went, in the off-licence, the draper's, the Mary Rose Tea Shop and over the privet hedges. So that when Mrs Culpepper rang me up to ask us round for drinks on Good Friday, I knew it was to thrash about in the subject yet again—though, adept at killing two birds with one stone, she barked, 'And tell Marcus to bring the stuff for Oscar's last injection,' before she banged down the phone.

When we got there, Franchita Culpepper was celebrating the crucifixion of Our Lord with a gin and tonic. Howard, her husband, seemed to have something beery tucked away somewhere, but he could only get to it in the intervals of being barman for everyone else. True, his services were not much called for by the Mipchins—she a dowdy, sharp-eyed creature of Scottish extraction, who ostentatiously demanded an orange squash, he a retired tax inspector with a Crippen moustache and a sense of humour, who was allowed to clutch at a single sherry that must have got warmer and warmer every time he took his occasional sips. Mrs and Colonel Weston, on the other hand, knocked it back cheerfully, the Colonel in particular, and so, I noticed, did Marcus, when he came in from the kitchen where he had been giving Oscar his jab. Both, of course, were getting up Dutch courage—something warming before the enemy attacked, a good solid breakfast before being hanged. We all settled down in the Culpeppers' drawing-room, stacked with the 'thirties memorabilia which they collected, and waited for the attack.

'You've been to see Mary?' barked Mrs Culpepper genially at Marcus. I rather liked Franchita Culpepper: she must have been a funny, sexy lady in her prime, and much of her bossiness now came from being bored. 'I hope she won you over?'

'Ah—you ladies! Always trying to win us over!' said Colonel Weston, in as feeble an attempt at gallantry as ever I heard. Mrs Culpepper shot him a glance of friendly contempt.

'Which means, I suppose, that you're intending to do damn-all about it?'

'I let Mary talk the thing through,' said Marcus, in his slow, comfortable way, which was his method of defusing a situation. It worked better, I always thought, with the animals of Hexton than with the human beings. 'I hope that she feels better about it now. I expect she was taking things a little too much to heart, after the death of her mother.'

'Poppycock,' said Franchita Culpepper.

'You seem to forget,' said Elspeth Mipchin (née Mac-Intyre) in her prim, still faintly Edinburgh tones, 'that there are matters of principle at stake.'

'Do you think so?' asked Marcus, puffing a veil of smoke around his face, perhaps to hide his expression. 'Surely we buried all that High Church–Low Church rivalry long ago, didn't we? I hope so, because it did us a great deal of harm. We're all Anglicans together now, eh, Colonel?'

'Eh? Oh yes, yes. All Christians too, what?'

There was a brief silence, as we sipped and considered this.

'I never did go much for this ecumenical spirit,' Franchita Culpepper said, at last. 'It always savoured of mushiness, you know. Everyone who went on about it always sounded so wet. The good old "Onward, Christian soldiers" spirit has always meant fighting other Christians, hasn't it? Give me a good fight any day of the week, rather than a warmed-up basin of ecumenicalism.'

'Blurring around the edges,' pronounced Mrs Mipchin, 'is positively dangerous, when there are matters of faith involved.'

'And are you hoping,' asked Franchita with heavy irony, 'that Mary is just going to let the subject drop?'

'I certainly hope that when she's thought things over a bit, and when she can get out of the house more, take up her old interests, she'll see that this isn't worth making such a fuss about,' said Marcus.

Franchita Culpepper's comment was a whoop of laughter.

'Hope springs eternal,' she said.

'What I cannot understand,' said Elspeth Mipchin, fixing the Colonel with firing-squad eyes, 'is why the position here was not made clear to the Bishop *in the early stages*.'

'Oh, Frank did his best,' loyally put in Nancy Weston, a fleshy lady with social pretensions, who made unwise attempts at a fluffy prettiness. 'After all, the Bishop is his CO, in a manner of speaking, so there are limits to what he could do. The Bishop's the one that in the last resort is going to lay it on the line . . .' She spoilt this spasm of marital solidarity by adding: 'Anyway, I never knew Frank convince anyone of anything.'

Colonel Weston held his peace. He had early on in his retirement to Hexton found out that if he spoke he put his foot in it, and I had rarely heard him say an unnecessary word in company. As a matter of fact, I knew through Marcus that what Colonel Weston had said to the Bishop was: 'Whatever you do, don't upset the women.' If the Bishop had consciously gone against this, it was no doubt for reasons of his own, and with the thought that it was up to the Colonel and the other lay dignitaries to fight their own battles with the women. Little did he know that they had long ago raised the white flag.

'And so,' summed up Franchita, 'due to the spinelessness of our menfolk—' she shoved forward her glass hand— 'refill me, Howard—we are to be landed with a celibate vicar. My God!'

'I never knew,' I said, to lighten the atmosphere, 'that sexual prowess was a criterion for promotion in the Church of England.'

Only Marcus laughed.

'The thing is,' explained Nancy Weston, 'that he's celibate *on principle*. That's what nobody quite likes.'

'Do you mean that nobody would object if he were merely celibate in practice?'

'Well, it would make it a damn sight more difficult to have a fight over it,' said Franchita, with that genial honesty that often endeared her to me.

'What I thought,' said Marcus, in his slow, country way,

'was that I would suggest to the Bishop that he send Father Battersby over to pay us a visit.'

There was an immediate pricking up of ears. Thus must the Bacchæ have pricked up their ears when they heard that Pentheus was in the vicinity.

'I thought that if he came here,' went on Marcus comfortably, 'and people could see he wasn't such a *rara avis*, and he could get to know us—well, then half the battle would be over.'

Dear, optimistic Marcus! But he had successfully defused the situation, I had to give him that—the situation, I mean, in Franchita Culpepper's drawing-room. The trouble with Marcus was that he believed that his defusings were longer-term than they really were, and that he had made the problem go away for good, when in reality it was merely quiescent, and waiting to erupt again with redoubled fury. For the moment, though, the combatants were silent, to consider their future conduct, and the men actually got in a few words together about the problems of the Yorkshire Cricket Club.

As a matter of fact, we drove over to Ripon on Easter Sunday, and after the service in the Cathedral Marcus went and had a word with the Bishop. I had taught ancient languages at a girls' school in Ripon, and I found plenty of friends to chat to after the service. So it was only that evening, after a substantial high tea, that I remembered why we had gone.

'What did the Bishop say about Father Battersby?' I asked.

'*Chariots of Fire* on television tonight,' said Marcus, leafing through the *Radio Times*.

'Oh God—high-minded athletes. Don't change the subject. What did the Bishop say about Battersby?'

'He said he'd heard that feeling among our ladies was running high . . . The Bishop knows our ladies.'

'Who doesn't?'

'He said he'd be happy to organize a visit to us by him . . . and he said he'd rely on me to see Battersby suffered no discourtesy while he was here. He said I was to make sure he wasn't victimized.'

'Ha! And how do you propose to do that?'

'I said if necessary I'd form a human phalanx round him of the churchwardens and sidesmen.'

'Ho-ho. A lot of chance you men would have if Mary and Franchita wanted to get at him. If they take against him, there's nothing on earth the Hexton males can do about it. They'll murder him.'

Later that evening, in bed, and on the verge of sleep, I drowsily said to Marcus:

'What *was* that book . . . by Ira Levin . . . about the community where the men had all their wives wiped out and lifelike dummies put in their places, who never contradicted, or made demands, or anything?'

'*The Stepford Wives*. I didn't think you liked the book at the time. Why?'

'It seems to me that what we have here is the Stepford husbands,' I said, going off to sleep.

CHAPTER 3

FATHER BATTERSBY

It was three weeks before Father Battersby could get away from his parish duties in Sheffield to pay us a visit. Marcus said that that would give us time to organize his reception, to make sure it was civil and accommodating. Ever the optimist, Marcus ignored the fact that it would give the ladies of Hexton time to organize as well, and that, good as he was at relaxing tensions, they were even better at screwing them up again—especially since Mary Morse had emerged from her mortuary purdah, and was organizing her campaign as if it were some sort of personal by-election.

I had had from the moment she first raised the issue misgivings about the new Mary that was emerging. The weeks leading up to Father Battersby's visit fully confirmed them. Dressed consistently in colours drab and dun (though of course she had never been a Mary Quant figure at the best of times), Mary scurried hither and thither around the town, assuming alternately an expression of brave bearing-up when anyone commiserated with her on her recent be-reavement, and one of eager-beaver determination when she was discussing the question of the vicar-to-be. Wherever one went shopping, at every social event or meeting, there she was to be seen, bearing down on some unsuspecting member of the Anglican congregation (sometimes so unsus-pecting that they were hardly aware that they *were* members of the Anglican congregation). She was, as they say, tireless —and how one hates people who are that! They are always, whether intentionally or not, mischief-makers, be they char-ity workers, schoolteachers or politicians. Mary was cer-tainly a mischief-maker, and she was it intentionally.

The only hopeful sign was that, like all such busybodies, Mary inevitably aroused opposition. 'What's she getting so het up for?' was a question often asked, or implied, and though the tendency of the questioners was of the quietistic or do-nothing school of behaviour (one suspects that some members of the congregation would have accepted a black mass on Sunday, provided the Satanist had been properly appointed by the Bishop), still, one did sympathize: who was Mary to lay it down as an immutable rule that the vicar of Hexton-on-Weir should have a wife? The opposition to Mary tended to be lower middle to working class, and to voice its opposition under its breath or behind its hands. Marcus was, in any case, not the man to use this opposition, perhaps wisely: it would make it too obvious, as he said, that battle lines were being drawn up. But, in spite of his scruples, battle lines there were, and we all knew it.

'I think we should do something for him,' said Marcus, one morning at breakfast.

'Do something?' I asked, knowing perfectly well what he meant.

'Have some people round in the evening.'

'I'm always happy to do that . . .' I said cautiously. 'Depending on the people . . . I am *not* having any fights about incense and thuribles in my living-room.'

'Oh, they wouldn't—'

'They would. You get all that over during the day, then we'll have some *nice* people round, and show him that some people in Hexton can behave in a civilized fashion.'

In the end, of course, the guest-list was a compromise, because Marcus was so good at quiet but stubborn insistence.

'I *won't* have Mary,' I said, when we got around to giving thought to actual names. 'I'll say to her that we'd *love* to have had her, but we know it's too *soon*. We'll have the Westons, because he's a sweetie, and she's all right if the others are not there to egg her on. We won't have the Culpeppers.'

'You like Franchita.'

'I do, but I can't control her, and in her present mood she'd bring faggots and burn the poor man in the back garden. If I hear she's going to be away I'll invite them. I'd like to have a talk with Howard, to find out if he exists. Same with the Mipchins, but she's never away, so we can forget them. I think I'll ask Mrs Nielson: she seems nice, she's new, and she doesn't know many people. Are there any younger people, I wonder?'

'I thought of that,' said Marcus. 'I thought we might invite Timothy and Fiona.'

'Oh God,' I said, 'isn't there anyone else?'

But as I said it I knew there was nobody else. Timothy and Fiona were Hexton's resident young people. Fiona was the Westons' daughter, Timothy the son of the Grammar

School headmaster. Just the mere sight of them together in the town square made people sigh and say what a lovely young couple they were—though they were not married, nor even, so far as I knew, engaged. Both of them were fair, anonymously good-looking, and they swanned it around Hexton like a Torvill and Dean begrounded by a universal thaw. Perpetually holding hands, gazing publicly into each other's eyes, greeting their elders with eager and courteous friendliness, they seemed like refugees from a 'thirties play, though their paraded courtship seemed to have lasted well beyond the regulation three acts. I found the performance quite stomach-turning, but I did not expect Marcus to share my feelings.

'All right,' I said, giving up with a sigh before the self-evident lack of alternative young people. 'Timothy and Fiona it is.'

'And of course we'll have to ask Thyrza Primp,' said Marcus.

'Marcus! No!'

'But we ought to, darling. As the widow of the former incumbent—it's something she'll expect.'

'Oh, expect, expect! She'll just sit there, Marcus, pursing her lips and saying things weren't like that in her Walter's time. She'll cast a blight over the whole evening.'

'She won't be with us long. You know, it *is* an attention she has a right to expect.'

'Couldn't she carry a load of high dudgeon with her into retirement at Harrogate? You could surely arrange for Father Battersby to call on her earlier in the day.'

'I think we'll have to ask her,' said Marcus, and I knew that was the effective end of the discussion.

The Primps had been carrying the banner of the Church Moribund in Hexton for as long as anyone could remember. He had become incumbent of St Edward the Confessor's round about the time of the Festival of Britain, though it seemed more like the Great Exhibition. Walter Primp, whom Mrs Nielson had charitably described as dull, had carried irresolution to a high art, and on all the great issues that had faced the Church of England, from the ordination of women to the remarriage of divorcés, he had dithered. But then so, of course, had the Church of England. His sermons were old-fashioned homilies on upholding moral standards, though it would have been extremely difficult to define what he thought those standards were. Thyrza Primp —well, you will meet Thyrza. Thyrza was about to retire to Harrogate, where many elderly people freeze away their last years. I could just imagine her icing over the pump waters, and curdling the cream on the cakes in Betty's Tea Shop.

'All right,' I said with a sigh. 'I'll ask Thyrza.'

It was very weak of me. I should have stood out against it. I think that on occasion, perhaps in reaction to Hexton ways, I veer towards the policy that Victorian wives adopted: let the husband take all the decisions, and then blame him afterwards. The fact is that though Marcus had the better understanding of principle, I had much the better understanding of people.

So that, as it turned out, was the line-up for the party: the Westons, Mrs Nielson, dear Timothy and Fiona, and Thyrza Primp. By dint of some tactful nosing around, I found that Franchita Culpepper was to be away (she made periodical visits to her dentist in Barnard's Castle, and was always away overnight, which made me very suspicious, though it had to be admitted that her teeth, like entrenched castanets, could be flashed with splendid effect for a woman of her age). Anyway, I asked them both, and Howard accepted for himself alone, seeming to wag some metaphorical tail at the thought of a run-around on his own.

'Don't put up with any nonsense from Howard,' said Franchita to me, sternly.

I did, I am afraid, make one big mistake, which I could not blame on Marcus. My formula for not asking Mary was,

I thought, rather clever: I stopped her in the street as she was buzzing round the town on her daily business of stirring up trouble, and I said that Marcus and I were having a party in the evening for Father Battersby, and I was asking her, though I quite understood, naturally, that this wasn't the sort of occasion she could go to, so soon after her bereavement. And Mary put on her brave smile, which was now as automatic as a mac in bad weather, and said how kind it was of me to ask, but *no*, she didn't think that . . . I went away congratulating myself on my combination of cunning and tact.

It was the day before Father Battersby's visit that Mary rang up and said she understood it was to be quite a *small* gathering—she'd got quite the wrong impression when I'd mentioned a *party*—and she felt she could manage just five or six, particularly as she so wished to meet *the Reverend* Battersby, and she so wanted Marcus to understand that there was nothing *personal* in her opposition.

I should have realized that the mourning etiquette of Hexton was a thing that could be subtly manipulated to suit individual convenience. I ground my teeth and added Mary.

The day of the visit dawned, and it dawned badly. Marcus had decided to take the day off entirely, and had delegated everything to Simon Fox, his junior partner. As always happened on such days, he got a call over breakfast from a farmer whose prize cow, with a complicated medical history that only Marcus apparently knew the ins and outs of, had gone down with a nasty bout of something-or-other that he said only Marcus could pull her through. The farm lay twenty-five miles north of Hexton-on-Weir. Cursing slightly, Marcus got out his car; cursing robustly, I walked towards the town square to meet Father Battersby.

He wasn't difficult to pick out when the bus drew in, that was one thing. None of this 'I'm just one of the chaps' informality that most clerics go in for these days. He actually wore robes—a cassock, or a soutane, or whatever the goddam thing is called. He was about thirty-five, I supposed, and while he was not good-looking, he was impressive in a gaunt, craggy, rather Victorian kind of way. He was a strong, determined man—if he had been a schoolmaster, the boys would have respected him enormously, and feared him not a little. In the 1840s one could imagine him renouncing all sorts of things for conscientious reasons—which presumably was what he had done in the 1980s, though today the climate of opinion rendered the renunciations ever so faintly ridiculous. From the start I liked him; from the start I thought what a nice change after Walter Primp to have someone who self-evidently knew his own mind and spoke it; from the start I knew that his coming would mean trouble in Hexton.

As I went round with him, desperately wishing Marcus would return from his silly cow, I became aware of something else which it is less easy to put into words. He was very slightly inhuman. He said the wrong thing, or he said the right thing to the wrong person. As a consequence he sometimes left people uneasy or resentful. I can illustrate this easily enough. I took him first to visit St Edward the Confessor's, down in its little hollow, and an attractive enough church to gladden the heart of a new incumbent. While we were there, Mrs Bates came in to freshen up the flowers, and naturally I introduced them, and they got talking. The conversation strayed around to a stint of three years Father Battersby had had in a remote mission in Tanzania. While he was talking about the disease and misery there, he was at his most intense: 'It makes me quite ill, when I remember all the suffering I saw in and around the place, to see how people begrudge making the least sacrifice from the absolute luxury we live in, to alleviate it.'

I saw Mrs Bates stiffen, the line of her mouth harden. Mrs Bates's husband had been declared redundant two years before, and had never found work; they had three children, and times were very hard for them. Of course, by any standards Father Battersby was right, and even Mrs Bates lived in absolute luxury in comparison with his remote Tanzanian tribesmen. And yet, one felt that another man might have noticed on her the signs of pinching and scraping —I could certainly see them, all too many of them, and one felt he ought to have been used to them in his parish in Sheffield—and would not have said that. As I say, I liked him; on any other occasion I would have enjoyed talking to him on my own, perhaps joshing him a little; as it was, I was pleased to hand him on to Marcus.

I had set the party at an early time. Father Battersby had to catch the 11.15 train to Sheffield from Darlington, and Marcus was to drive him there, so I'd said seven o'clock. I'd prepared a buffet supper, so that everyone could perch how and where they could, even in the garden if it was fine. It wasn't a very Hexton way of doing things, but I certainly couldn't seat so many round my dinner table. Promptly at two minutes past seven the doorbell rang, and there stood Timothy and Fiona, looking all scrubbed and eager and dewy, as if they had been auditioning for roles in a particularly tepid soap-opera. Just behind them came the Westons, Fiona's parents. Nancy Weston was one of the leaders of the 'Aren't they a lovely couple?' brigade; Colonel Weston, on the other hand, I had sometimes caught casting glances at Timothy that were charged with something very close to suspicion.

Then they all started coming: Mrs Nielson arrived almost simultaneously with Howard Culpepper. She had, by arrangement, brought Gustave ('I know other people's dogs are a pain, but he does bark when I'm out and annoy the neighbours'), and we put him up in our bedroom. Then Mary arrived, with a conspicuously sober demeanour, like a Roman virgin at her first orgy of the season. She was terribly and unremittingly sweet to everyone. Then Marcus and Father Battersby got back from calling on the town's oldest communicant, with whom Father Battersby, it seemed, had been a great success (he reminded her, apparently, of what 'the cloth' had been like in her girlhood, and she kept looking at him and saying 'That's more like!'). And then, lastly, came Thyrza, bringing with her—not by arrangement but pretty much by tradition—her dog Patch.

Patch was a Jack Russell. At bottom he was a rather nice-natured dog, I was convinced, but at top he was a highly aggressive yapper. He formed quite a fitting accompaniment to Thyrza Primp, but in her case I was much less sure of the nice nature at bottom. We put Patch in what we called the nursery, destined for children who had never come, and scenting the presence of Gustave and my dog Jasper in the vicinity he created merry hell for about ten minutes, and then settled down for a bit of shut-eye.

Thyrza, meanwhile, had been accorded the armchair of honour in the sitting-room while she had graciously allowed me to settle her dog. She sat there, her short, squat body encased in a tight black dress of a hideous crimply material, her black eyes drilling slowly and painfully through one person in the room after another. On her lap was a handbag, clutched tightly with both hands, as if she were in Sicily. The bag snapped open—'Primp!' I always heard it say—and snapped shut, and at moments when she wished to express shock or disapproval she would snap it open—Primp!—take out a tiny embroidered handkerchief, raise it to her nose, and sniff. Then she would return it to her handbag—Primp!—and sit staring fixedly in front of her. This was Thyrza Primp, wife, helpmeet, taskmaster and terrorizer of poor dead Walter. As Mary kept saying, what would we do without Thyrza? Soon, praise God, we were going to find out.

I managed to busy myself in the kitchen, so as not to worry too much about the ill-assorted guests and how they were shaking down with each other. On my trips in and out ferrying food I noted that Father Battersby was in a little group with Mrs Nielson and Howard Culpepper, which seemed a way of letting him down lightly. Howard was doggy and enthusiastic, and getting in opinions from time to time, which Franchita would doubtless have said was very bad for discipline. Mrs Nielson was being apologetic (in a manner Father Battersby had no doubt heard countless times before) about the half-heartedness of her Anglicanism.

'I used to work in a hospital, and of course I saw all the good work done by priests there, when people were in trouble, or dying, or often just generally by coming and talking to them; but I'm afraid I got into the habit of thinking of them in that way: people for special occasions —often very unhappy occasions.'

'You're far from alone in that,' said Father Battersby. 'That's one of the tasks of the Church today: we're not integrated into the *whole* of people's lives . . .'

It was standard churchy chat. No doubt something similar was going on around Thyrza Primp, for there in a dutiful and duty-bound group were collected Marcus and the Westons, all bent forward over her in a vaguely deferential manner, as if she were a distinguished visitor who would shortly be asked to snip a ribbon or push a button. On the other side of the room Mary stood talking to Timothy and Fiona, who were holding hands on the widow-seat, smiling innocently, and looking as if someone ought soon to bounce in and invite them to make a foursome at tennis.

When the buffet was set out I summoned everybody to take a plate and a fork and to help themselves to whatever they liked. Marcus meanwhile attended to their alcoholic needs from bottles which he had most dishonestly filled from wine-boxes. Mrs Nielson enthusiastically heaped her plate with hot and cold this-and-thats, and then, thinking that she had monopolized Father Battersby enough, she got herself into a corner with the Westons. The rest of the party were less sure what to do: '*awfully* pleasant and informal,' said Mary, with the clear implication that something a *little* more starchy would have been more considerate to her bereaved state. They all took little bits of one thing, and kept having to come back for more. It was difficult to marshal them into sympathetic groupings, and in the end I realized that Mary had landed up with Father Battersby. Well, it had to happen during the evening at some stage. Mary, I saw, was leading the conversation with an expression of sweet forbearance on her face. I was sure that she was demonstrating to Marcus that there was nothing *personal* in all this. I was also sure that this was a mere overture, before she got down to the nitty-gritty.

I, for my sins, went to do my duty by Thyrza Primp. That was weak of me, for I should have let Marcus stew in his own juice. Thyrza had procured for herself the boniest available piece of duck and a small spoonful of rice salad, and she sat picking at it with an air of martyrdom, the handbag still perched on the cliff-edge of her knees. I squatted on a stool beside her, and attempted to keep the conversation clean. To no avail.

'Have you noticed,' said Thyrza Primp, after suffering a bare minimum of my polite inanities, 'what that young man is wearing?'

Since long black robes are not normal social wear in this day and age, one could hardly help noticing.

'Probably awfully convenient,' I said brightly.

'Walter, naturally, would never have had any truck with suchlike nonsense, but it's called a soutane.' She lowered her voice to a menacing hiss. 'And I think you'd find, if you counted, that the buttons down the front number thirty-nine!'

'Would I?'

'Symbolical.'

'Really? What of? The steps?'

'The Articles!' Thyrza snapped open her handbag— Primp!—and sniffed at her handkerchief, a sniff that managed to unite in condemnation both Father Battersby and me. When she snapped her bag shut I jumped, as if my nose had been caught in it.

'I call it blatant superstition,' Thyrza resumed. 'Childish and trivial. I must say—' with a significant sigh—'I begin to be eager to remove myself to Harrogate.'

'I'm sure you must be,' I said in my bright, neutral voice.

'Harrogate, I believe, has *many* churches, so that one can *choose* the sort of service that *suits* one. And good congregations, too.'

(Those dying generations, I thought.)

'To have remained here, to have seen Romish practices imported, to have seen all Walter's wonderful work go for nothing—it would have been too painful!'

'I suppose one always does feel like that when there are changes,' I said, feeling a right little Pollyanna.

Over by the fireplace, Mary and Father Battersby seemed to have got to the nitty-gritty. There was definitely something in the nature of an inquisition going on. Happily Mary could hardly broach the subject of Father Battersby's disinclination for intercourse, but I did hear words like 'incense', 'chasuble' and 'surplice', and Mary's expression had changed to that of one discharging a burdensome but necessary social duty. I was interested to see the manner of Father Battersby's response: he replied directly, in a friendly way, but totally without apology or any attempt at ingratiation. I suspected, too, that there was not a hint of compromise. I caught Marcus's eye, smiled at him brilliantly, and shifted my eyes fractionally in the direction of the fireplace. What hostessly perfection! Marcus got up and went over to the fireplace, to make it a threesome.

After a time the groupings began to loosen up. People went back to the table for more food and drink; some of them began eating it standing up, so they could circulate and find pleasanter or at any rate different company. Some even went into the garden to talk to our dog Jasper, who is a genial soul who welcomes any company, and to feed him scraps. Howard Culpepper was getting on very well with Mrs Nielson and eating voraciously of everything on offer (surely Franchita didn't keep him *hungry*?). Mrs Weston was flirting fluffily with Marcus, who was becoming quite avuncular (Marcus had the bulk and geniality for avuncularity, and with a few extra years would have made a good Prime Minister in the Callaghan mould, or a good telly performer when vets came back into fashion). As the evening wore on, Father Battersby spoke to everyone in one or other of the groups, and to most of them singly, for long periods or short. I began to think that the opposition was not going to have it all their own way. His directness and patent honesty were winning people over. For example, I thought that Mrs Weston might be won over to support her husband more vigorously, and to side with the choice of the ecclesiastical powers-that-be. Her daughter Fiona also seemed very taken with him, and this meant that Timothy volunteered the opinion that he seemed a 'jolly nice chap'. Mrs Nielson had been disposed to like him in any case—on the same grounds that I had: that he seemed likely to relieve the monotony. What line Howard Culpepper would have taken had he retained a mind of his own and the right to form opinions I do not know, but he kept mum, merely skipping friskily from group to group, uttering inanities and enjoying his temporary freedom.

It was inevitable that at some time in the evening Father Battersby would have to have 'a good talk' with Thyrza Primp. Typically, he had had no thought of giving her precedence, but by ten-fifteen he had realized that the thing had become urgent. He moved over to the armchair in which she had sat throughout the evening, like Queen Victoria in widowhood reluctantly holding a levée at Windsor. Mrs Nielson was the present recipient of her graciousness, if that was the word (for she was being glared at for lighting up a cigarette), and he joined them quite naturally. But from the beginning he showed that he was determined (having suffered one inquisition) to keep the chat on neutral lines.

'It's certainly a fascinating, beautiful town,' I heard (by dint of moving nearer) him say. 'Just walking round it today with Helen and Marcus has been an eye-opener. You could say it has cast a spell over me. Is that what the "hex" in Hexton means, I wonder—a benevolent spell?'

'Oh no,' said Mrs Nielson, eager to keep the conversation friendly. 'I believe it's a Scandinavian or German word for "witch"—the town of the witches.'

As soon as she'd said it she blushed and looked confused. As well she might. I moved a step or two away to hide my laughter. What a perfectly apt name: the town of the witches!

'Well, burning witches is one old custom I've no desire to see revived,' said Father Battersby, determinedly pleasant. 'I think bazaars and fêtes provide a much more healthy form of entertainment in a parish. By the way, I've accepted Marcus's invitation to come here a week earlier than I intended, so that I can attend the church fête in June. I'm looking forward to it.'

'You have decided, then,' enunciated Thyrza Primp, in a voice like a trumpeter warming up for the Last Trump, 'to accept the appointment?'

Father Battersby turned to her, with ingenuously open eyes.

'Oh yes, Mrs Primp. I never was in any doubt about accepting.'

'I see,' said Thyrza. She drew in a deep breath, and I realized that she was about to launch into a sort of credo. 'My husband,' she pronounced, as if launching into a funeral eulogy, 'believed in moderation. In trying to avoid giving offence. He saw the dangers in strife in a parish, and he looked for the middle way and then took it. Undeviatingly.'

'I'm sure he did an excellent job,' said Father Battersby. I noticed that soothing nothings sounded unconvincing from his lips, and I'm sure Thyrza noticed too.

'It was so with the services as well. Walter didn't try to be controversial in his sermons, like so many of these modern clergymen. Nor to bring in a lot of heathen pageantry. We had a sober, reverent, decent form of service here, with nothing extreme, because that was what suited the people of Hexton.'

'I'm sure you did,' said Father Battersby. 'You must not take any changes I make as in any way a criticism of my predecessor.'

'Changes! I don't think you'll find people want any changes. We don't go in for fads and novelties here! Walter suited Hexton because he knew the people don't run after change. They know the value of moderation. How often I remember Walter saying it, in the pulpit and out: "Moderation in all things."'

'Don't you think moderation in *all* things might in itself be a sort of excess?' asked Father Battersby.

Primp! went the handbag. Out came the handkerchief. Sniff! This was an outraged sniff, combined with a wounded sniff. It was a crisis point, and Thyrza pushed her long nose forward into the hanky for a second sniff before she returned it—Primp!—to her bag. She set her lips, fixed her eyes to drill needle-thin holes in the wall opposite, and said not one word more. Mrs Nielson covered up, Father Battersby played along, but Thyrza Primp squatted on there, silent, grim, implacable.

'Well, time we were on our way to the station,' said Marcus, a good ten minutes before it was necessary. Father Battersby nodded goodbye to Mrs Primp, tolerably certain that a proffered hand would be refused. Then he went round to farewell all the other guests. Mary was extremely polite, almost gracious. The Westons asked him to stay when he came for the fête, but he said he was going to stay with the Blatchleys (an interesting decision that, almost a political one: the Blatchleys were not social leaders in Hexton, he being a mere bus driver). Howard Culpepper said they'd have to get together for a drink some time. Timothy and Fiona were found to have made their excuses to Marcus earlier in the evening and gone. Marcus got him out of the front gate, into the car, and drove him away—thankfully, I have no doubt, and promising himself a stiff whisky when he'd done the duty driving.

Inside, the rest of the party began to show signs of breaking up. Mrs Nielson was in the hall, and shouting 'Coming now, boy' to Gustave, which set Patch off into a machine-gun rattle of barks, which in its turn set Jasper off on the back lawn. The Westons collected their coats, but Howard Culpepper said he'd just have one for the road, if I'd join him. He seemed to be savouring every moment of freedom. I smiled and said I fancied a last drink myself, and we turned into the living-room.

'Boycott!' came Mary Morse's voice, firm, and quite lacking in the social softness which it had had during the foregoing evening. 'It's the only way. An organized boycott of the church as long as he is the minister there!'

She was standing by Thyrza Primp's armchair, and over their heads I seemed to see fluttering in a breeze a garish ensign of war.

CHAPTER 4

BATTLE LINES

I never did have that talk with Howard, to find out if he existed. Or rather, we had the talk, but I gave it only half my mind, because over on the other side of the room a plan of battle was being drawn up. When the two of them left, they had prim little smiles of anticipation on their faces. Howard Culpepper muttered, 'Looks as if we're in for some rough weather,' and scuttled in their wake. I think he'd taken one look at my face and seen I was in no mood for the harmless flirtations of the elderly that I suspect he went in for when he was allowed out on his own.

I told Marcus when he returned, and he did something that he very seldom did: he totally lost his cool. He is one of those very quiet people who on a handful of occasions in their lives simply blow up. I suspect if Mary had been to hand he would have blasted her up hill and down dale, and reduced her—yes, even Mary—to tears and submission. As it was, he put on a pretty impressive performance *in vacuo* for my benefit, so that I didn't even rub it in that it was he who had insisted on inviting Thyrza Primp. The level on our bottle of Johnnie Walker plummeted like the falling pound, and Marcus finished the evening, as he so often did when something had whipped up his comfortable surface, by playing Beethoven's Pastoral (in his normal moods he said it presented an intolerably prettified view of the countryside). Even when, long afterwards, he went to sleep, it was a disturbed and unhappy sleep.

I often said to Marcus that his religion was inherited. This was quite unfair, for his religion was deep-rooted and sincere. It was his busy-ness in Church matters that was inherited. His father was a schoolteacher and churchwarden who, to his family's surprise, took orders late in life and died in a small parish in the Midlands. Marcus had spent all his life, from choirboy days on, doing things in and for the Church. It was impossible for him now to wash his hands and say that things would have to take their course; that Father Battersby was the Bishop's appointee, that he, Marcus, had done all he could to make the appointment acceptable to Hexton-on-Weir, and that now they'd just have to see how things worked out. It just wasn't in Marcus to do that. The next morning, after surgery, he went to have it out with Mary.

I heard about the interview in a somewhat fragmented fashion. By chance I met during the morning an old colleague from the High School in Ripon, and we arranged to have lunch in the Chinese Restaurant. We were deep in the menu, and Mr Li was bending over us and indulging in his 'You like sweet-sour plawns?' talk (outside the restaurant he spoke broad Australian English, but he claimed it disconcerted the tourists if he did it at his place of business, so he maintained a cheerfully split personality); and thus we did not notice when Mary and Thyrza Primp came in and took the table next to ours. The restaurant, by the way, was quite half empty. When I looked up I'm sure my face revealed my displeasure. I'm equally sure that this pleased Mary, who felt she had somehow made a point. She leaned across to me, with a brave smile that was adapted from the one that was part of her funeral mien.

'Your Marcus has been most unkind to me today,' she said. 'He accused me of making a great fuss about trivialities. I wish you could make him see that matters of faith are not to be characterized as trivial. Especially by one who is a churchwarden.'

I smiled in steely fashion, and turned back to my friend without a word. I'd had Mary Morse. Mary and Thyrza, ostentatiously *not* lowering their voices, began talking about hiring a bus every Sunday to ferry the orthodox to St Mary's, in Shipford. This project, which became known to the amorphous opposition to Mary's doings as the 'God bus' or the 'Godmobile' later became the subject of much ridicule, I'm pleased to say.

Marcus told me a little more that evening.

'I told her that she'd got too little to do, and she was filling up her time by making a great fuss about nothing . . . I think I also said she was a bit of a trouble-maker, and that she should stop thinking of herself as the keeper of the town's conscience.'

'Not bad,' I said, 'though erring on the side of mildness, as usual with you. Did you actually lose your temper?'

'I didn't explode in a great fuss-fumble, if that's what you mean,' said Marcus, with a grin. 'I lost it enough to give her a piece of my mind.'

'I saw her later, so I won't bother to ask if it had any effect.'

'I did extract a promise that when Father Battersby came for the fête, he would be courteously received.'

'A fat lot of good such a promise will be,' I said dismissively. 'Courtesy comes in a variety of temperatures, particularly for Thyrza. She lowers her temperature automatically for Methodists. For Father Battersby it's going to feel like solitary confinement in Siberia. You realize that in the Chinese restaurant today they were discussing laying on a bus to Shipford every Sunday?'

'Damn those women!' shouted Marcus, banging his pipe down on the fireplace so hard that he broke the stem. 'If Mary wants a fight, I'll fight her! I'm going to make sure the man is properly received, and has a congregation to come to!'

'Hmmm,' I said. 'I should start organizing one of those armed bodyguards American presidents have if you want the man to see sunset on the day of the fête.'

The fête, you notice, was now beginning to loom large in the calendar of Hexton's Anglicans. It was always the big event in June, held in a marquee on the meadows beneath the castle. Marcus had suggested that this year I might organize it, but I had jibbed. I am not a pillar of the Church of England, merely a minor buttress. Thyrza Primp could not do it, being occupied with moving her snuffy odds and ends to the happy haven of Harrogate. Mary, in her bereaved state, could not, since a fête was essentially festive (though remembering some of the earlier Hexton fêtes I had been to, I felt this argument had very little weight to it). Thus the job fell to Franchita Culpepper and Mrs Mipchin. Franchita returned from her visit to the dentist like a giant refreshed, and repolished. She threw herself into organizing the event with a ferocious energy that was quite terrifying, and would have been excessive if she had been arranging the Edinburgh Tattoo. Wheedling, cajoling, threatening, bullying, everything was done in a tremendous whirl, and up and down the wynds of Hexton people began to shrink inside the doorways of their old stone houses when they saw Franchita coming. Mrs Mipchin burrowed along industriously in her wake.

I was beginning, in fact, to find Mrs Mipchin useful. I, inevitably, was involved in a minor way with the fête. I call it a fête, but it is really a mixture of bazaar, bring-and-buy sale, and fairground. There are outdoor games and indoor games, to provide for both kinds of weather, and stalls selling all imaginable kinds of things, from baby clothes to homemade coconut ice. The aim of the sensible attender was to get rid of a lot of his own unwanted rubbish, without acquiring any of somebody else's, but you had to be really strong of mind or short of purse to manage that. The outdoor games were mostly macho affairs of the trial-of-strength kind, by which the local boys and the lads from the army camp vied with each other to impress the local girls. The indoor ones were more varied. Last year I had run a roulette-type game that had brought a faintly wicked whiff of the casino to Hexton. This year, so as not to associate the pro-Battersby party with even the faintest suspicion of moral laxity, I opted to run the 'Antiques and Nearly' stall with Mr Horsforth, the Grammar School headmaster, father of the ineffable Timothy. This was, of course, the junk stall, and as everyone said, 'It was surprising what you could pick up' (if you weren't careful). Anyway, in the run-up to the fête, I was on occasion thrown into the company of Mrs Mipchin, and, as I say, she proved useful.

She was a woman totally devoid of humour. She made Mrs Thatcher sound like a stand-up comic. Rigid, narrow-minded and dull, she walked all her days veiled in the dreariest garb of propriety and respectability. So totally incapable was she of detecting irony that I found I could drop into the conversation suggestions for the most outrageous courses of action for the anti-Battersby party. Provided these were not reported to Franchita (and Franchita was busy for much of the time, hallooing up hill and down dale, lassooing in helpers and netting home produce of all kinds), these suggestions might get straight back to Mary or Thyrza Primp, who were similarly devoid of humour, and then be seriously canvassed. I would say, 'I'm surprised Mary doesn't get up a petition to British Rail to reopen the station for a Sunday service to Shipford.' Or: 'Of course the Archbishop of Canterbury is the ultimate court of appeal.' The fact that Mary and her committee could so gravely discuss such absurd ideas resulted in a great deal of rough bucolic scoffing, and did great harm to their cause.

I was enlisting myself, you notice, into the Battersby cause. I suppose I did so for Marcus's sake, and because I so detested Mary Morse and Thyrza Primp. I had certainly liked Father Battersby (though in general I prefer a more comfortable sort of man), but I had a suspicion that he would not thank anyone for organizing support for him. I rather thought he felt he could carry off things perfectly well on his own account when he took up the living.

So that was the position as the day of the fête approached. On the one hand stood Mary, Thyrza, Franchita, Mrs Mipchin, and a band of like-minded souls, well- or ill-meaning. I would not want you to think that the tide was turning against Mary. Hexton was a town afflicted with a kind of mental sciatica, and most of its inhabitants were always two or three steps behind everyone else. Change of any kind being suspect, they were not likely to welcome the new ways and views that Father Battersby represented. Nor were they any too bright: I came to believe that the word 'celibate' conjured up for them all sorts of steamy but ill-defined images that made them wonder how he could have managed hitherto to keep out of the Sunday papers.

On the other side there stood Marcus, Colonel Weston,

and a large, amorphous group of people who had no particular feelings about ceremonial versus evangelical plainness, or indeed about celibacy, but who resented being dictated to by a middle-aged, middle-class woman who arrogated to herself the right to set the tone for Hexton. This group, as I say, was amorphous, but they looked into each other's eyes and recognized their fellowship. Marcus did as little as possible overt recruiting, but the Blatchleys, with whom Father Battersby was staying for the fête, were more shamelessly drumming up support, so that experts were predicting that Father Battersby's first service would have the largest congregation seen in Hexton for years, and the most working-class. It was all mildly exciting, as well as decidedly amusing.

One day in late May, a week or so before the fête, I was walking Jasper on the path around the castle. Hexton Castle is in ruins, or nearly so, and of course it looks much better that way. The path is high and shady, with precipitous descents down to the weir, and a fine view of the meadows. The descents meant that I had to keep a sharp eye on Jasper, which I have to do in any case: he is a dog of quite undiscriminating sexuality, who is liable to throw himself on top of dog, bitch, squirrel or fox. He is a lovable black mongrel, an RSPCA £10 Special Offer. Marcus never said so openly, but he was upset by the cruelty involved in a lot of dog-breeding. Anyway, mongrels are healthier, and he said he was damned if he was going to spend his home time physicking his own dog.

The first person I met on Castle Walk this particular day was Mr Mipchin—he of the Crippen moustache and the much-suppressed sense of humour. It was nice to think he had emerged from his career as a tax man with no manic passion about Clause 94, subsection 23A (iv), and that there might lurk a real and quirky person somewhere there, if only he were allowed out. On this occasion, he actually nudged me in the ribs.

'I suspect you're being naughty, Mrs K,' he said, his moustaches bobbing up and down like walrus leaping for fish.

'Why, Mr Mipchin,' I replied, in traditional style, 'whatever can you mean?'

'Having my good lady on is what I mean. And all the other good ladies too.'

'I don't think I know any good ladies,' I said.

'"Unco, guid", as my wife's fellow-countryman once said. I suspect you're leading them on! Well, I must say, I like a good blow-up. All adds a touch of spice to life, eh? eh?'

And he toddled off round the curve, chuckling asthmatically. Another secret sympathizer, I thought; another member of the underground resistance, terrified into apparent submission by Hexton's SS.

Amusing myself with the thought of how much *secret* support Father Battersby would have by the time he arrived in Hexton, and wondering whether any of it could be harnessed into action, I walked on from the precipitous paths around the north wall of the castle, and down the pleasanter slopes back towards town. And the next person I bumped into was Marcus—standing near the steps down to Castle Wynd, and talking to my partner-to-be on the junk stall, Mr Horsforth.

I knew Mr Horsforth quite well, because I am on the County's list of supply teachers, and I quite often have had spells filling in at the Hexton Grammar School (as we still called it, though the powers-that-be had altered it to something more democratic-sounding). Mr Horsforth was tall, bony, authoritarian and fond of the sound of his own voice. He gave the rest of the world the feeling that they would have trouble living up to *his* standards. 'Silly little boy' was his favourite expression of rebuke to his pupils, and he gave teachers the impression that he would like to say something similar to them. As I said, Timothy—he of the fair hair and the long, loving fox-trot around Hexton with Fiona Weston—was his son, and on the infrequent occasions when I felt charitable, I had to admit that the role could not have been an easy one. He had had a wife, thin, wispy and self-effacing, but she had slipped out of the world apologetically some five or six years before.

I let Jasper off the lead to romp around the castle slopes with Smokey, Mr Horsforth's humorous Old English sheepdog, who, like Jasper, was a dog of rampant sexuality. I watched them for a moment, like a voyeur, then I joined the men.

No prizes for guessing what they were discussing.

'She is being incredibly childish,' said Mr Horsforth, in his thin, precise voice. 'Stirring up trouble, driving the town into opposing camps, and generally behaving like someone in a Victorian novel. Somebody should tell her.'

'I have,' said Marcus. 'You could try doing the same, if you liked. It's like banging your head against the Tower of London.'

'I'm afraid she wouldn't acknowledge *my* having any right to lay down the law for her,' said Mr Horsforth, his voice regretful of human perversity. 'I suppose the only one who might have done that was Walter Primp.'

'And he was too weak to try,' I put in. 'Mary and Franchita and Co. get away with murder because nobody stands up to them.' I looked up towards the castle walls, where Jasper was giving a new meaning to the song 'On Top of Old Smokey'. 'Oh, Jasper—*really*!'

'Smokey! Here! At once! Heel! Heel, boy!'

Mr Horsforth, having demonstrated his authority over his dog, in default of being able to do it over Mary, smiled thinly at me and went on:

'I'm not sure there is a *great* deal I can do for you, Marcus. As you know, I'm rather an occasional churchgoer—' (That was true. Mr Horsforth came three or four times a year, and sat through the service with an air of believing that religion was an excellent thing for the troops, but it mustn't be thought that *he* believed such nonsense.) 'Insofar as I *am* a member of the congregation, I'm against all this sectarian silliness, so I'm entirely with you there. Beyond that . . .'

'One thing you can do, on the day of the fête, is help me ensure that he's given a courteous reception. But beyond that, I hoped you could find one or two interested boys to introduce to him. You know that the Lads' Brigade and the Youth Club and all that sort of thing fell away long ago—Walter *wasn't* an inspirer, poor man, especially of the young—and I know Father Battersby is hoping to revive them. Young people, I imagine, are likely to find Mary and her antics wildly old-hat and ridiculous, and if you could say a few words, perhaps at assembly, about the dangers of bigotry and intolerance (not tying them in in any way with the current situation, of course), and if you could get together a nucleus of the sort of lad that you think might be interested, and might give a hand to Father Battersby, then I think the ground would be properly prepared for him, and all this opposition seen in its true perspective.'

'I could perhaps do that. There *is* a type of lad who is predisposed to the religious thing.' (This last was said as from a great height, and certainly put Marcus in his place.) 'And I can detail my boy to give a hand with anything this Battersby starts up. There's bound to be a good turn-out of boys to the fête, and I can get Timothy to round up a few of the more presentable ones and take them along to him. I'll take him round and introduce him to a few people, if needs be. In the intervals, of course, of peddling near-antiques with your good lady.'

'Thyrza's junk,' I said. 'Stuff too awful to be taken to Harrogate. I think we'll work on a system that as soon as either of us has sold five items of Thyrza's junk, we've earned fifteen minutes off.'

Mr Horsforth smiled thinly, his bow towards a sense of humour.

'Well, good day to you, Marcus. Good day, Helen.'

And he allowed Smokey one last roll with Jasper, and then they proceeded in an orderly manner up the path.

'I'm not sure Mr Horsforth is someone I'd choose as an ally,' I said, watching him go.

'He's not someone I'd care to go out for a drink with, that's for sure. Still, he's a useful man in some ways.' Marcus took my arm, and we went back towards town. 'And give him his due: he's too sensible to go along with any of this bigotry that Mary is peddling around the town.'

'What makes you think,' I said suddenly, 'that Father Battersby is any less bigoted than Mary?'

'Oh, surely not, surely not. Anyway, if he is, we'll face that problem when we come to it.'

That was Marcus—a great one for facing problems when he came to them.

CHAPTER 5

WATERY BIER

The day of the fête dawned bright and clear, as they say in children's books where it always does. Hexton-on-Weir was seldom so lucky, though it would have been wrong to blame entirely for the dismal atmosphere the drizzle or squally showers with which the town was usually favoured. People had a lot to do with it too. This year, though, the sky was pure blue from early morning, and the sun played on laburnums and lilacs and early roses in the Hexton gardens.

'No one could make trouble on a day like this,' said Marcus, tucking into a hearty plateful of bacon and eggs that was designed to make him forget food for eight or nine hours.

I marvelled at his optimism, particularly in view of the fact that he'd been warned. Thyrza Primp had been along to the surgery two days before with Patch. She wanted Marcus to give him a general check-up, apparently to see if he could stand the excitements of Harrogate. When Marcus tried to give her his little lecture on charity, tolerance and open-mindedness, she said that in her view (and in that of poor Walter) the Church had been a good deal too open in recent years, and it was time to remember that we were not Methodists or Romans but Anglicans, with our own ways. She regretted the necessity of making it clear to Father Battersby that he was not wanted in this parish, but she felt that the need to impress this on him fell to her, in view of her position in the parish, and she did not intend to shirk it. He would be left in no doubt of the feelings of the town towards him. 'We shall do it in the politest possible way,' she added ominously.

By the morning of the fête Father Battersby had been in Hexton for about twelve hours, and I hoped he had suffered nothing worse than a snub from Thyrza or Mary. He had stayed overnight at the Blatchleys', and in fact was to stay there until Thyrza moved out of the vicarage on the following Saturday. Marcus was sufficiently involved with the fête to have arranged no special meeting with him, beyond saying that he would meet him there. We both, in fact, were busy enough, in all conscience, from early in the morning. Marcus was helping set up the outdoor games and trials of strength, in preparation for the opening, which was set for eleven o'clock. I was organizing the vast array of junk we had collected for display on our stall, which was carefully situated in one of the best and most central positions in the marquee (good, it must be said, for chatting to people, as well as selling things). I say 'our' stall, but I had collected the stuff, and now I was being allowed to set it out—Mr Horsforth merely standing by and saying 'You do it so well.' The implication that this was 'woman's work' seemed to hang unspoken in the atmosphere.

If there is anything I loathe, it's being watched while I'm

working. I said: 'I hope you've organized a few presentable boys to meet Father Battersby?'

'Heavens above, it quite slipped my mind,' he fussed. 'Timothy! Timothy!'

Across the chaos of preparation in the marquee a fair head turned readily in the direction of the call. Mr Horsforth fussed off, and I saw him giving lengthy and peremptory instructions to his son. I wondered, idly, how many young men of twenty-three or -four would like being summoned and instructed in that manner by their father in a public place.

I turned my attention to the junk. I call it junk because the majority of the stuff was Thyrza's. I had, in fact, been able to pick up one or two good pieces of this and that from other people, but Thyrza's junk surrounded me in cartons: whereas she would have had to pay the garbage men to come and cart it away, I not only had to collect it myself, but also to feign gratitude as well. *And* Thyrza would throw a fit of bad temper when she saw that not all of it was displayed. That was out of the question, however. I devoted one end of the stall to a selection of the stuff: souvenirs of depressing holiday-resorts, a stone hot-water bottle, a monstrous collection of hatpins, odd shoe-trees, moth-eaten tablemats, a broken brass fender and a Britannia metal inkwell and penholder. Still in the cartons was a bedpan. I thought of labelling that end of the stall *Souvenirs of Thyrza Primp*, but I did not think that her popularity with the public at large was such that they would want any keepsake of her after she had taken herself into her chilly retirement. The better things were given a better display at the other end of the stall, and I had a few of those in reserve, too, as soon as any of them should go. I priced them high. On Thyrza's things I was ready to negotiate a give-away.

Across the aisle I noticed that Mrs Nielson had priced all her homemade jams and chutneys at 40p.

'Too cheap,' I shouted.

'No it's not,' she shouted back, patting Gustave, who was tied up under the table. 'It's rubbish, most of it. Why should people pay the same price as for good commercial jams, or more? I tell everyone that of course *theirs* was lovely, but not everyone's was, and I couldn't cause ill-feeling by setting different prices . . .'

Mrs Nielson seemed to be getting Hexton's measure (though she was wrongly dressed: her powder-blue suit and hat were that bit too formal and old-fashioned for the fête, since that is the day when Hexton women celebrate the coming of summer in flowery skirts and cotton blouses—if it's not raincoats and wellies weather).

It was getting close to eleven o'clock, and soon it would be time for the raging mob to be let in. A brief trip outside the marquee (to get away from the babble, which was o'ertopped by the constant loud-hailing of Franchita, who was at her most bossy and unreasonable, and might have been masterminding D-Day) suggested that today there would indeed be a crowd. The sun had brought them out, and old and young were beginning to congregate in the meadows, casually dressed, good-humoured and flirtatious. Just the crowd to be indulgently disposed towards the home produce stall, the candy-floss bar, the knitwear stall, the Bingo drives, the Test the Power of Your Grip machine, the tea and coffee stall (with exorbitant prices) and the home handicrafts display: Just the crowd, too, to listen indulgently to the efforts of the Hexton choir, which was even now assembling outside to present its first musical offering of the day. The Hexton choir existed to sing *Messiah* at Christmas, and to try, if possessed by an adventurous mood, to put together a performance of *The Creation* or *Elijah* at some other point of the year. The only time they had attempted a modern work, they had made *Belshazzar's Feast* sound like Belshazzar's tea-party. Now they launched themselves, with that predictability that characterizes local do's of this kind, into 'Sumer is icumen in'. I stood in the sun, looking up to the winding town, to the castle and to Castle Walk, and thought that Hexton was not such a bad place to live in after all. Thus does Hexton woo one, delusively, from time to time. I saw Marcus getting his substantial bulk behind a hefty mallet, and trying to ring the bell on the Test Your Strength machine (he very nearly made it, as he very nearly made it each year). Then I saw Father Battersby arriving.

He was coming with the Blatchley family, from the direction of Chapel Wynd, where they lived. There were three Blatchley children, noisy and energetic, and ranging in age from five to fourteen. Each of them had gathered around them a little knot of friends, and the parents, pleasant, popular people, had also accumulated acquaintances as they walked. So, though they did little in the way of formal introduction, Father Battersby had already a little circle round him, and he shook hands with some, exchanged words with others, and I saw no sign that his—what shall I call it?—his slightly abstract sympathy, his difficulty of seeing things in purely human terms, had resulted in any of those unlucky coolnesses that I had seen on his previous visit. Probably he was better when he felt at home. It was all pleasant, informal, appropriate, and it gave me some inkling of another Hexton that I wished I knew better.

'Failed to hit that damned bell again.' It was Marcus, coming up behind me. 'Still, I was no further off than last year. I say, that's Father Battersby, isn't it?'

'I can't imagine there's likely to be anyone else at the fête wearing that gear.'

'Perhaps I'd better go and welcome him.'

'Don't. Let it happen naturally. It's all quite spontaneous and informal at the moment, and I think it's better that way.'

As I spoke, the Blatchley and Battersby party were approaching the marquee, and the town clock over the square struck eleven. As if by magic, the substantial figure of Franchita appeared through the flap in the marquee.

'Roll up! Roll up!' she shouted with fearsome gaiety, as

she pushed back the flap. When she noticed the approach of the Battersby party her jollity stopped dead in its tracks: one could almost see contending in her face the duty of inflicting a snub, and the desire not to mar the beginning of 'her' fête with unpleasantness. In the end, what I like to think of as her good nature won out, and she stepped forward to meet the party, her hand outstretched.

'Welcome to Hexton-on-Weir . . . Father.'

Father Battersby smiled, nodded, shook hands, and passed in. I slipped through the flap and raced to my stall. Mr Horsforth, naturally, was nowhere to be seen, though I could hear his voice through a mêlée of helpers. The Blatchley party came in, in the wake of the new vicar, then a mere trickle of others, then more and more. The Annual Hexton Church Fête had begun.

The first hours of a fête are usually the busiest, and this one was no exception. The fête worked up to a kind of climax around lunch-time and drooped rather thereafter. I certainly had my hands full, because Mr Horsforth's appearances behind the stall were so spasmodic as to be almost token. He irritated me a great deal and had I not been to some extent dependent on his goodwill, being a possible supply teacher, I would have said something sharp, never finding it difficult to find something sharp to say. I was quite willing to believe that a headmaster had more duties to fulfil and more people to have a word with than the wife of a vet, but in that case why volunteer for duty at all? Meanwhile it was I, on my own, who had to cope with the rush of customers.

Mr Mipchin was one of my early buyers, and one with a good eye. Among the better things that I had accumulated or wheedled out of people was a charming mid-Victorian tea-caddy, which he took a fancy to. I pushed him up to a good price, and insisted that he take something from Thyrza's stuff as well. He chose a little model of a lady in Welsh national costume, holding a broom, and in her dusty and decrepit state looking tolerably like a witch.

'Something to remember her by,' he said, and I could swear there was a malicious little smile playing around somewhere underneath the walrus moustaches.

Thyrza's stuff usually met with an incredulous rummaging, with a racking of memories among the eldery to dredge up the purpose of this or that item. 'Egg cosies!' they would say contemptuously. 'Who on earth uses *them* these days?'

'Cor, look, Annie,' said one fat lady, the wife of one of Hexton's greengrocers. 'A toasting fork! And hatpins! She could never have used all them hatpins. And remember them things, Annie? They called them chafing dishes in the olden days.'

'That's very cheap,' I said determinedly, for it was one of the more saleable items. 'You should buy it as a souvenir of Thyrza Primp.'

'Best souvenir I can have of *her* is the sight of her back when the bus leaves,' came the dour reply. So much for 'dear Thyrza', so irreplaceable, in Mary's eyes, in Hexton life.

Father Battersby, meanwhile, was going around, meeting people, having a word here, a nod there, and generally seeming to need no outside help in getting to know people. I was glad Marcus had made little effort to arrange anything, because what was happening was so obviously unpremeditated. I never saw him but that he was surrounded by one or two, or by a little knot. Timothy, I noticed, obedient to his father's detail, brought along periodically some schoolboy or other to have a shy word with the new vicar. (What Timothy's father was doing with the time he was *not* spending at the stall I had no idea.) When Father Battersby got round to my stall, I had some new experience of his talent for the *mal à propos*. By chance Mrs Mipchin was standing at Mrs Nielson's stall opposite, having her sandalled toes licked disdainfully by Gustave, and examining pots of strawberry jam to try to avoid the runniest. ('They're all a *bit* runny,' Mrs Nielson was saying dubiously, 'but I expect it's just the heat.')

'Hello, hello—I still haven't thanked you for your hospitality last time I was here,' said Father Battersby, in his carrying, clergyman's voice. (He hadn't, either. That was one of the little formalities that I suspect he set little store by.) 'Golly, what a collection of this and that you've got here. Where does it all come from?'

'That's all Thyrza Primp's,' I said, neutrally. 'Stuff she's clearing out of the vicarage, to let you in.'

'Yes,' he said, gazing down at the pile. 'As soon as one moves, one realizes what an awful lot of rubbish one has accumulated.'

It wasn't much, but it was enough. I heard, even over the babble of the crowd, a sharp, shocked intake of breath; when I was conscious of Mrs Mipchin's sandalled feet scurrying away, I had no doubt where she was going: straight to the vicarage and Thyrza, to retail it, with many a tut-tut. But Father Battersby had moved blithely on, and just then Mr Horsforth reappeared, so that I could take the opportunity (as I realized I had to, on his rare visitations) of snatching a break.

Outside the stuffy, sweaty tent, the atmosphere was pleasanter. True, I was unlucky enough to witness the arrival of Lady Godetia, even as I took my first breaths of fresh air. Lady Godetia did not open our fêtes (it was said because she was too lazy to get up that early, and spent too much time making herself up), but she closed them with a gracious speech of thanks to the helpers which I always tried hard to miss. Lady Godetia was chronically gracious, like royalty at the end of a particularly gruelling tour. She was our local gentry—in fact the widow of Sir Frank Peabody, who had been something in packaging, but also the daughter of some obscure Earl whose interests in life had been exclusively horticultural. She passed into the marquee, smiling a smile of weak honey, and I stood there, hoping that she would have got round to my stall and expended her graciousness on Mr Horsforth before I went back in.

Otherwise it was lovely outside. The marquee was set fairly close to the river, and a breeze flowed welcomingly along with the stream. It was a regular place of resort on any sunny afternoon, and today there were many couples in swimsuits by it, some just lying, some bathing tentatively —for it flowed fast from the weir. Such as these were not likely to come into the marquee, but they were now and then tempted by the outdoor games, which were doing famously. Marcus was boyishly cock-a-hoop.

'Only three have rung the bell so far,' he said, 'so I didn't do badly, for an old 'un.'

'Such vanity,' I said, 'at your age.'

'It's at my age that vanity sets in. How are things going in there? How is Father B. doing?'

'Splendidly, so far as I can judge. Meeting hundreds of people, and everyone pleased to meet him.'

'So whatever it was that Mary and Thyrza were planning, it hasn't come off?'

'Mary and Thyrza,' I said, in a mock-ominous voice, 'have not yet arrived.'

Back at my duty-station behind the junk stall, I parried Mr Horsforth's reproachful look with a bright smile. After a moment or two of looking much-put-upon, he made a rapid departure with scarcely a mutter of apology. I soon understood why: Lady Godetia approached, in company with Franchita, the pair of them looking like a gracious yacht in the custody of a man-o'-war.

'*Awfully* pleased to see you again,' oozed Lady Godetia, with a brilliant, generalized smile. 'Weren't you running some kind of frightfully amusing and wicked game last year?' (She kept us all card-indexed, I was convinced of it.) 'And your husband is the terribly attractive vet who's been out to see to my horses. *Such* a charming man—you should keep him under wraps if you don't want him stolen! And what have you got this year? . . . *Such* an interesting jumble of stuff. What a delightful screen! You're not going to let me have that cheap, I suppose?'

Her greedy eye, peering through the piles of Max Factor, had alighted on a pretty little hand-embroidered screen placed among my better things.

'Fifteen pounds,' I said.

'Ah well, no, I *thought* you wouldn't . . . *What* an amusing collection you have here. Things you hardly ever see these days. Hatpins, for instance—you never see those.'

'Nonsense,' said Franchita brusquely. 'Depends on the hat. Damned useful in a high wind.'

'15p each,' I said. 'Six for 50p.'

'Ah well, then, I *might*,' said Lady Godetia, who spread her patronage, like her graciousness, thinly. 'Perhaps I'll take *two*.'

She was counting out 30p, mostly in small change, into my hand when I noticed that Mary Morse had arrived. In a dress the colour of fog over Birmingham she was standing at the end of our row, clutching a handbag, and surreptitiously letting her eyes dart everywhere. It soon became clear what she was looking for. Father Battersby was at the moment passing between my stall and Mrs Nielson's stall, accompanied by Timothy and Fiona, who looked as if they were advertising some aid to personal freshness, and three schoolboys, who didn't. Whatever they were talking about, he was giving his all to the conversation, and as Mary approached along the aisle, her face set in a stony expression, her eyes staring straight ahead of her, as in a prison photograph, I wondered whether he was going to notice her at all. I think in fact he did, but did not remember her. Certainly he passed her, still listening to one of the grubby schoolboys, and showing no sign either of recognition or of registering a snub. Mary's prim little mouth contracted, her eyes clouded over. Then she came up to my stall, noticed my amused eyes watching her, turned in my direction the coldest of cold shoulders, and greeted Lady Godetia— sketching, I swear it, a sort of suggestion of a curtsey, a half-bob. They bustled off together, all condescension and fawn, and soon were deep in conversation. Mary and Lady Godetia served on several committees together in the town, on which they did a great deal of quiet harm. Their energetic talk was probably about persuading the librarian only to buy 'nice' books for the library. Lady Godetia had a taste for innocuous pap, and Mary was the sort who still finds Thomas Hardy controversial.

Watching them go, I raised my eyebrows sky-high. Mrs Nielson, observing everything from across the way, giggled. Franchita said, 'Now, Helen—' but she rather looked as if she'd like to give way to her braying laugh too. Then she bustled off energetically to organize something—anything.

'What time are you going for lunch?' shouted Mrs Nielson, over the heads of some customers.

'Heaven knows if I'll get any,' I said.

'I certainly intend to have some.'

'Have you got a stand-in?'

'No. I'll just put a sheet over this lot.'

'But people will pinch them.'

'Surely not. But good luck to them if they do. I signed up for voluntary work, not slave labour.'

The idea of lunch was very attractive. I was beginning to drop on my feet. Voluntary work *did* have a habit of turning into slave labour.

'Franchita will be furious,' I said dubiously.

'Let her. As soon as your man puts in another appearance, we'll scoot off to the Chinese.'

'No—that I *wouldn't* dare. But we could pick up some sandwiches from the stall and eat them outside.'

Meanwhile Mr Horsforth was nowhere to be seen. The crush of people was at its height, but most of my good things had gone, so as people rummaged through Thyrza's rubbish my attention could wander. By now Thyrza had also arrived, chugging bleakly around the place like an ancient tug destined shortly for the scrapyard. Passing my stall, she cast black looks at the amount of stuff still unsold, and picked up something that looked like (but I'm sure was not) some primitive piece of contraceptive equipment.

'Now I thought that would be *sure* to go,' she said reproachfully, and then put it back and steamed heavily ahead.

Her ill-humour was marvellously augmented by the scant success of her and Mary's intention publicly to snub, pointedly to ignore, Father Battersby. So crowded was the tent, so surrounded by people was Father Battersby, that he was proving unsnubbable. Really, there *was* something a little inhuman about the man: after all, anyone else entering a living would feel it necessary, or would find it courteous, to pay public attention to the widow of his predecessor. Father Battersby felt no such compulsion; or else he felt that, after the encounter at ours, it would be best for all concerned if he avoided further meetings with Thyrza Primp. So she and Mary could march up the aisles he was proceeding along, they could fix him with long-range, unseeing stares, they could turn icy shoulders, sniff as if they smelt gas leaking —it all went for nothing. Father Battersby chatted, listened, stopped to buy, and was apparently quite unconscious of their presence. It was like an old regime giving way painfully to a new. And if Father Battersby did not notice the antics of some members of the old order, others did, and rejoiced at their discomfiture.

'Silly women,' came a voice at my back, as I witnessed one such non-encounter. 'Silly, silly women.'

It was Marcus, come in for a ten-minute break from the mallet and the bell.

'Forget it. They're not getting through, and it's doing them no good whatsoever. Who's testing their strength?'

'Weston. He's taking over entirely at three-thirty. Then

I'm going home for a cup of tea and a pipe in the peace of my own armchair. Coming?'

'No such luck. Would that I could. I'm stuck here until all this junk goes. And Mr Horsforth is damn-all use as a partner.'

'He's a busy man—I expect he has lots of other things to do,' said Marcus comfortably.

'I have a lot of other things to do, but I don't get to do them,' I said resentfully. 'Are you coming back later?'

'Oh yes, of course: I'll be here for the finish.'

'For Lady Godetia and her "absolutely magnificent effort on the part of all concerned"?' I said, amused by Marcus's inbred stickling for doing the right thing. 'That's when I shall take off. I'll go home and prepare you an absolutely enormous dinner—a steak the size of a plate.'

We stood there in companionable silence, letting the fête flow around us. Marcus noticed the arrival of some slightly tipsy soldiers from the barracks, and he kept his eye on them for any sign of their causing 'unpleasantness'. Marcus could never abide unpleasantness. I really rather liked it. I grinned secretly as I listened to the subterranean mutterings and grumbles around me: 'She had the cheek to charge . . .' 'Charity's one thing, but I don't like being done! . . .' 'It's not a chutney I'd expect anyone to pay good money for; and then she goes and gives me 20p too little change . . .' 'I mean*say* . . .'

Our brief moment of intimacy, hands held under the stall, was ended by Mr Horsforth's breezy and unapologetic reappearance.

'Right!' I said briskly. 'Mrs Nielson and I are going for lunch. I can't stand here in this heat all day without a bite to eat, or I'll faint.'

'I've only had a cup of tea and a scone myself,' protested Mr Horsforth.

'Well, that's a cup of tea and a scone more than I've had. Come along, Gwen.'

Gwen Nielson had got distracted by a lost child, a tiny mite, howling and blubbering for its mother. She was on her haunches, comforting it with nonsense talk. When she saw I was at last free, she held it up over the crowd, called 'Anybody own this little lad?', delivered it over to a not-noticeably-grateful parent, then shoved a sheet roughly over the few jars remaining on her stall and made off with Gustave and me to the sandwich bar. Really, she was a very capable woman.

With a few packages of standard fête fare, we pushed our way outside. The crush on the meadows was beginning to diminish, and people were wandering home to late lunches, or to get a drink in before the pubs closed down for the afternoon. Down by the river there was a group of five or six soldiers, noisier than the ones inside, who had been jolly and good-natured. These had clearly been getting their drinks in since the pubs opened. We took ourselves as far away from them as possible, and sat on the cool grass in a far corner of the meadows, eating the regulation ham sandwiches. Gwen Nielson fed Gustave with cooked meat she had brought in a bag—his yaps for the next bit, meticulously timed, being the only disturbances to our peace.

'Well,' I said, 'it seems to be going well this year.'

'Is this what you call going well? Financially I suppose —even my stall: I had ninety-seven jars to start with, and about eighteen are left. Say eighty jars at forty pence—I make that thirty-two quid. And even then Franchita will say I should have charged more. But I can't say it's my favourite sort of occasion: I'm standing there thinking I'll make sure and take my holidays in early June next year. Too many people, too much bustle.'

'Well, better busy than dismal,' I remarked, with uncharacteristic optimism. 'We've had some pretty dire occasions in the past, as you can probably imagine: if it wasn't because of the weather, it was because of the people.'

'At least Miss Morse and Mrs Primp don't seem to be succeeding in damping anyone's spirits.'

'Aren't they incredibly childish? And all *simply* to make trouble—simply to get a bit of excitement into their lives.'

'Certainly I can't see one priest being replaced by another making *that* much difference to Hexton life,' agreed Mrs Nielson, lighting up a cigarette. 'Of course, Mary says she owes it to her dead mother . . .'

'Ha! No doubt Queen Victoria said she owed it to her poor dead Albert when she was intent on doing something particularly selfish and disagreeable . . . Oh God, let's forget Hexton and its doings. When are you going on holiday this year?'

'I don't know that I'll have one. Too soon after the move here, which was really rather expensive. And I'm not sure of the best place to go, now that I have to decide for myself.'

'Was your husband the type who did everything for you?'

'I don't know. Not consciously, perhaps, but he was a doctor, and in fact his word was mostly law. Oh, Gustave —be quiet!'

But Gustave, having finished up all his meal, was determined on a walk. He had a splendid confidence about getting his way, and no doubt he felt it his due, after having been tied for so long to the leg of the stall. Gwen Nielson stubbed out her cigarette and took him off, he barking rapturously at having made his point. I lay back in the sun and closed my eyes. Now, if I was sensible, I'd take twenty minutes off and enjoy a little snooze. It was really quite pleasant here, almost peaceful, apart from the distant shouts and songs of the drunken soldiery. And, really, Mr Horsforth had *not* pulled his weight so far, not by a long chalk. I really ought to leave him to get on with it . . .

But of course I didn't. What is operating in such cases I don't know—my conscience, Marcus's conscience, or what —but my pleasure rarely gets the upper hand over my duty, and my duty assumes ridiculous forms. I dragged myself back towards the tent. People were showing the exhaustion that overcomes Englishmen after quite a small amount of sun. Father Battersby, though, was still spry, enjoying a picnic with the Blatchleys down by the river. At the Test Your Strength machine Colonel Weston had apparently taken over from Marcus, and his 'lady wife' (as he often called her, and to which term, incredibly, she made no objections) was apparently intending to stand fluffily by him and offer admiring remarks to the local youth (who in fact had more flab than bicep under the sleeves of their T-shirts). I greeted them casually, and passed into the tent and out of the sunshine.

The Hexton choir was putting in their third stint of duty that day, exhorting everybody to climb every mountain. The crowd was definitely thinning now. At my stall Mr Horsforth had disposed of little of the remaining stuff. He looked at me reproachfully and made off—as if we had come to some sort of arrangement about shift working, and I had somehow reneged on it. I ground my teeth and smiled compassionately at the rummagers around my stall. Now the crush was over one could see all sorts of things that one hadn't noticed before. Howard Culpepper had a stall of second-hand jigsaws and games only two stalls down from my own, but I hadn't registered him all day. Par for the course with Howard, of course. A good quarter of the stalls were sold out, though mostly their keepers lingered round them, either because they were terrified of Franchita, or because they did not want to forgo the gracious thanks of Lady Godetia. Mrs Nielson, on the other hand, had only five jars of jam left, and when she had sold these, she locked up her cash box, packed up and left, in spite of my warnings about the wrath of Franchita.

I wished I could do the same. There were still three cartons of junk behind the stall, and still latecomers trailing in and contemptuously turning over Thyrza's things, in default of anything else much worth buying. We were paying the penalty of success, and the day was quite early wearing an enervated, faded, stale-end sort of air. Outside, no doubt, was better, and the games and sideshows would be flourishing as the weather got cooler. I breathed in the stale air and wished I could get out. A tent on a wet day was bad enough, but a tent on a hot day was pure hell.

Suddenly I noticed that others seemed equally possessed by a passion to escape the tent. Or at any rate, down at the far end the area around the entrance that gave out on to the meadows and the river were almost empty. The people down that end—attracted, presumably, by something I had not heard—had gone out, and were standing around outside, whispering to each other.

The people around the junk stall had noticed too. 'What is it?' they said to each other. 'Must be something happening.' And they started to drift in that direction. I was pricked by the needle of curiosity, and the desire to escape into the fresh air. When there was no one in front of my stall, I nipped over and retrieved the old sheet that Gwen Nielson had used at lunch-time. I threw it over the remaining junk, and then darted down to the other entrance, which was still uncrowded, and then out into the open. The freshness of the late afternoon air was wonderful. I breathed it in two or three times, and then walked round to the other side of the tent, and to the river.

It was the river they were all looking at. Floating down it, propelled by the currents of the weir and kept afloat by a hefty branch to which it had become attached, was the body of a man. I ran forward to the river bank, though someone—Colonel Weston, I think—had put out a hand to hold me back. From the bank I could see clearly: the dark green tweed jacket; the old flannels; above all the jaunty little hat with the feather which had somehow clung to the branch, and which he always wore to these do's. Which Marcus always wore to these do's.

CHAPTER 6

CURTAINS

You will not, I imagine and hope, have set me down as the fainting type. But from the moment of that sight until perhaps an hour later I have no memories—only *feelings*: a feeling of being loaded gently on to a stretcher; a feeling of being somehow in my own house again; a feeling that an ice-cream van was playing outside, and that it shouldn't be, leading to a drowsy consideration of whether I hated the one that played 'Greensleeves' more than the one that played the Harry Lime Theme or the one that played '*O Sole Mio*', ending with a lazy decision that I did. When I had come, solemnly, to that conclusion, I opened my eyes, and saw the light and the lampshade in the ceiling over my own bed, turned and saw the bold patterned curtains drawn across the windows. It was then that the memories began, and the pain.

'She's coming to,' I heard a voice say. It was Dr McPhail's voice, my own GP. I sensed his shape approaching the bed.

'Helen, I'm going to give you a sedative. I want you to have a long sleep. The nurse will stay with you.'

I pushed myself with painful slowness up in the bed, looked at him, and shook my head.

'No.'

'Helen, I know you don't like taking orders, but this time I want you to do as I say.'

'It's true, then? He's dead?'

'They brought the body in a quarter of a mile down river. Yes, I'm afraid he's dead.'

I stared ahead, and a great wave of grief, bitterness and anger swept over me. Marcus—the gentlest soul alive, the warm, quiet, loving man who had been with me in this bed for twelve years. I did not want to share my grief with these people, and I did not want to have it sedated out of me either. I did not even want to know how it happened, merely to come painfully to terms with the *fact* that it had, and the feeling of black emptiness that it left me with. Yet even as I thought this, something inside me said: Marcus was not the type to fall into rivers and not be able to get out again.

Dr McPhail left me alone for a few seconds, and then approached again with his glass.

'Now, Helen—'

I waved him aside.

'Harold, if you will go away, both of you, I promise you that I'll rest. You can look in again if you want, say about nine or nine-thirty. But I won't take anything to put me out.'

Harold McPhail looked at me. He knew my reading tastes, and it did not surprise me when he quoted: "The highest calling and election is to do without opium . . ."

'And its delusively attractive modern equivalents,' I said.

'But I wish you'd let Nurse Burwash stay.'

I looked at Nurse Burwash. She was a nice enough soul, but she always reminded me of a policeman in drag.

'I'm sure you understand, Nurse. I have to be alone.'

So in the end they went, and Dr McPhail left his damned sedative by the bed, instead of inside me, and I lay there crying my grief into manageable order for some time. In the end, all the memories and the love reduced themselves in my mind to one simple proposition: Marcus had been such a *living* person. Not lively, but so largely involved in life, getting such pleasure from it, putting himself so generously back into it. Not mourning for the things he didn't have —children, for example—but getting such an immediate satisfaction out of the things he did have. And that warm, comfortable presence—smelling, as often as not, mainly of animals and tobacco—had been cut out of life.

Why did I use that expression 'cut out of life'? I think in my mind I had been going through all the alternative possibilities and rejecting them, though quite subconsciously. I went through them consciously now. I knew Marcus's mind, and his faith, too well to even consider suicide. An accidental slipping into the river, followed by an inability to get out again, I had already rejected: Marcus was a strong swimmer, and generally capable on a physical level. The only possible scenario I could imagine was something like a heart attack while he was standing on the river bank (the path was a couple of feet from the bank, so he would have had to have been standing on the very verge). Marcus was of course coming up to the age of heart attacks, though in fact his heart, and his health generally, was strong. Gradually there had stolen into my brain the conviction that it was not God who had struck him down, but man. Or perhaps more specifically woman. Hexton had got him. He had been deliberately, wantonly sheared off, as a vandal might cut at living blooms, because their naturalness offended him. I understood now the graveyard words staled by use: 'cut down in his prime'. I had been denied the years I should have had with him.

I then did something very illogical. I went slightly uncertainly downstairs, and I poured myself a small whisky. So much for doing without opium. I went back to bed, and lay there sipping it, and thinking ahead to the next stage: how had he come to be in the river? Who had killed him?

The first image that came to my mind was Marcus, almost the last time I had seen him alive. He was standing by my stall, listening to the din and the talk all around him, but looking at a party of tipsy servicemen who had just come into the tent. My brain struggled with memories rendered fuggy by my faint. That was the *less* drunk of the two lots of servicemen: the group outside had been louder and nastier. Had Marcus in fact gone to 'do something' about them? He dearly hated unpleasantness. Had that hatred brought upon him the greatest unpleasantness of all?

But I put the idea from me. If he had remonstrated with them near the tent, there would have been crowds around to see him go in the water. If, on the other hand, the servicemen had left the area of the meadows—and the body had obviously been floating for some time down from the weir, to judge by the crowd that had collected to watch it— then there would have been no reason for him to remonstrate with them, since they would not be disturbing the fête. In any case, I put the idea from me for another reason: I believed it was Hexton that had killed Marcus. The service-men were, on occasion, brutal and rough enough, but they were not murderous. And they were not in any real sense Hexton.

Yet, when it came down to it, the body that one might have expected to see floating down the river was not Marcus's, but Father Battersby's. Admittedly there was something about the Father that repelled the ultimate familiarity of murder. Just as he had sailed serenely through Mary and Thyrza's ambushes and attempts at snubs, so he would have fixed his would-be murderer with that determined eye, and forced him to drop his weapon. So, at any rate, one felt. Perhaps Marcus was in a sense a second-best choice.

Yet Marcus, too, was in his way an unlikely murder victim. Not that he had that spiritual steeliness that Father Battersby possessed: Marcus was another type altogether —cosy, accommodating, approachable; he saw good in everyone, and let it be a source of wonder to him that everyone in his world could not be friends. And yet Marcus was a formidable bulk of a man to murder: tall, burly, physically confident. Certainly I'd have backed him against three or four of those drunken soldiers. Did this mean, then, that the blow, shot, or whatever it was, was unexpected? Was he *shot*, perhaps, totally unawares? Yet who in Hexton, apart from Colonel Weston and a few more or less competent grouse-shooters, could one visualize handling a gun?

I had finished my whisky. I felt drear, heavy, yet totally clear-headed. I put the glass down on the bedside table, swung my legs from the bed to the floor, and stood up: a little groggy now, no more. I had promised Dr McPhail to rest, not to rest until he came. I walked downstairs, more confidently this time. I took one of my rare cigarettes from the box on the mantelpiece and lit it. Then I did something very strange: I took from the 'fridge the steak I had been saving for Marcus, and put it into a pan and fried it. I threw together a salad, and then I sat down and ate ravenously, cutting and wolfing at it again and again. I suppose this will seem heartless—a sort of symbolic eating of Marcus out of my life. I only know that all these steps back to normality were helpful—did not make my grief less, but put it into a controllable shape. They also made me more and more determined that Hexton would pay for what it had done to Marcus.

The attack on Marcus was probably unexpected. I had got that far. Yet how small a way that really was. Because Marcus would never suspect anyone of murderous designs on him. Short of the killing occurring in the middle of a stand-up fight with knives, Marcus would not conceivably have anticipated being killed. And I didn't think he had got into any fight with knives. I thought he had got into a conversation with one of the upright burghers of Hexton, and in the course of it had been killed. What had it been done with? How had the weapon come to be so readily to hand? And what had the talk been about?

As I chomped hungrily through the large steak, the Marcus-sized steak, I projected a scene on to the screen of my mind. On the way home, walking along by the river—but why *that* way home? The longer way?—Marcus meets one of our pillars of the community. They engage in conversation, and in the course of it Marcus upbraids him (her? almost certainly *her*) about the happenings of that afternoon. The conversation becomes rancorous, and the other person—

There my invention lagged. And in any case, re-running the scene in the cinema of my mind, I found it less than satisfying, or rather less than convincing. Though Marcus had been apprehensive about the fête, in the event it had gone off swimmingly from his point of view. Would he then, in his euphoria, willingly open up the subject with any member of the opposition? Would he so gratuitously cause an 'unpleasantness'? That went quite against Marcus's nature, his habits of conciliation. Of course if the other party had opened up the subject . . . Then it would have to be someone so stupid as to be insensible to the shame and ridicule that the afternoon's fiasco had brought on them . . . There were candidates for that role.

Then there was the question of opportunity. There the mind began to boggle. That I had remained aware of the comings and goings in the tent earlier in the day was true, but by the time Marcus must have been killed, things were becoming very hazy indeed. And even though the fête tent was becoming less crowded, it was still perfectly easy for someone to be there without my knowing. Mr Horsforth, for example, when he wasn't at the stall (as he mostly wasn't), could have been down by the tea-and-coffee table, or outside around the Test Your Strength games, and thus have a perfectly good alibi that I could know nothing about. It was going to be difficult enough for the police to establish alibis in a setting of constant comings and goings, and it was quite impossible for me to. There was nothing to be gained by thinking along those lines as yet.

I was startled by a ring at the door. It was Harold McPhail, come back to see how I was. I led him through into the dining-room, and when he saw the nearly-eaten steak on a plate the dear man did not even raise an eyebrow. But I, new in that twilight world of the newly-widowed, felt the need to excuse myself.

'I somehow needed to get back to normality,' I said. 'Or to some version of it.'

'You don't have to explain to me, Helen. I haven't been a doctor for twenty-five years without knowing that people find their own ways of coping with sudden death. There's nothing unnatural about being hungry, whatever the circumstances. But some people prefer sedation, I can assure you, and there's nothing unnatural about *that* either.'

'I'm sorry. You think me arrogant. Perhaps the sedation will come later,' I said, more humbly.

He sat himself down at the dining table.

'I don't know the details, Helen, but he was killed.'

'Of course he was killed,' I said abruptly. 'Sorry. But there was no other possible explanation, was there?'

'You don't mean you know who might have done it?'

'Good God, no. I meant that he could hardly have got in there accidentally. And if there's one thing I know about Marcus, it's that he was not the suicidal type. That's ruled out both by temperament and by religion. Someone killed him—but as to who had motives . . . Of course, there's been all this unpleasantness recently about the appointment of Father Battersby, but I find it difficult . . . After all, it's all so *trivial*, isn't it?'

Harold McPhail smiled.

'I can imagine you would think so. You're not really a wholehearted churchwoman, are you, Helen?'

'I'm an agnostic, converted by marriage rather than reason,' I admitted. 'Still, even if I were passionately involved, I can't see myself getting *that* het up about one kind of vicar rather than another. I mean, you'd have to be a pretty funny kind of Christian to murder for your point of view, wouldn't you?'

'Other things get involved,' said McPhail.

I sat there thinking about that for a while, toying with a piece of lettuce.

'True,' I said at last. 'Other things like vanity, hurts to your sense of your own importance. That's the only way I can make sense of this—as the result of wounded vanity.

Some nasty little worm of conceit that couldn't bear to be defeated and humiliated . . . But I still think that Father Battersby would have been a more likely victim.'

'I was only at the fête briefly,' said McPhail, 'but I wouldn't have thought that Father Battersby was a very get-at-able victim, from what I saw.'

'No,' I admitted. 'He certainly wasn't.'

'What the police are going to want to know,' said McPhail, looking at me thoughtfully, 'is where everyone was.'

'I know. I've been trying to think of that myself. What sort of time is it they're interested in?'

'From about three onwards. Until the time he—'

'Was seen floating. Yes. I understand. The trouble is that it's all so chaotic in my mind. The fête was beginning to wind down then. I *think* Mary was still around at about three, but I can't be sure. Thyrza I hadn't seen for quite a bit . . . Mr Horsforth was conspicuous by his absence most of the day. Whereas Franchita was conspicuous by her presence. She was lady of the fête, and was here, there and everywhere most of the time. I can't believe it could be her, because I think we would have noticed if she had let up for the time it would take . . . Timothy and Fiona were swanning it around in their non-stop Bolero, and I kept seeing Timothy with Father Battersby, but I noticed them most during the morning . . . Mrs Nielson sold out and went home . . . The Mipchins were in and out, but the Westons were mostly with the outside games, so I don't know about them . . . It's all so *difficult*.'

'When I said that the police would want to know where everyone was,' said Harold McPhail carefully, 'I really meant that you should try to remember where *you* were.'

I looked up at him, and suddenly I flushed bright red as a spurt of anger flashed through me.

'Oh, my God! I see what you're getting at! You mean that the police will see me as the prime suspect! Christ! I only need that!'

As I marched to the mantelpiece to get another cigarette, Harold McPhail said:

'I didn't say you would be the prime suspect. But obviously you will be among those that they have to consider. You don't stand outside the investigation just because you *know* you didn't do it.'

'Oh, I've got the idea now,' I said, bitterly. 'In murder cases of a domestic kind, the husband or the wife is always top of the list. You're quite right: it's something I ought to be aware of. I just thought that anyone who knew us—'

'The policeman will not have known you. He won't be a local man. And how many of us *really* know others?'

As he spoke the telephone rang. Still flushed and angry, I marched to pick it up. All I needed was to hear, down the line, the hushed tones of Mary Morse.

'Helen? Dear, this is not the time for condolences, but I thought you'd like to know that you've forgotten to draw your curtains. A friend just walked past your house, and she commented—'

'God damn and blast you all to hell,' I said, and banged down the receiver.

CHAPTER 7

COLD STEEL

So livid was I at Mary's phone call, so anxious was I to get things moving and to worry the police into activity, that I nearly rang them then and there and suggested that I talk to them the same evening. I can't account for this needling itch for activity, except that I seemed to need it to push the darkness back further. I think, too, that I was saying to myself that as soon as the case was solved, I was going to shake the dust of Hexton-on-Weir off my shoes and depart

I knew not where. Anyway, Harold McPhail persuaded me that it would be most unwise: I was too het up, I would say things I would regret later and give the officer in charge a misleading impression. And anyway, he said, the official medics would hardly have put in even a preliminary report by then. That clinched it: I wanted to know exactly what had happened. However, after Harold McPhail had gone, I rang up the Station and fixed a meeting for ten o'clock next morning. I said I was quite willing to go to the Station, having no intention of retreating into the sort of purdah Hexton deems suitable for the first weeks of widowhood. But the Detective-Superintendent on the case said it would be helpful for him to talk about Marcus in his own home, so that was what we arranged. I felt prickles of hostility against the man, convinced he had marked me down already as a prime suspect, but I had to admit that his voice sounded businesslike.

I spent a night during which sheer exhaustion sometimes sent me off into a fitful sleep, but which otherwise was a matter of tossing and turning, grieving and wondering, and most of all a tormented nagging the subject over in my mind which got me nowhere, but left me exhausted and fretful. The next day dawned like a yawning hole—the loneliness, the purposelessness opening up before me in all their blank horror. I was alone.

And the police were coming. I boiled an egg, and ate it with bread and butter. I lit a cigarette, but after a few puffs decided I wasn't going to go down *that* road, and stubbed it out. I put on some coffee for myself and the policemen. I thought they probably would in fact prefer instant, and then I cursed myself for such a snobbish, Hexton thought. Whatever happened, I was not going to become Hexton.

When the Detective-Superintendent on the case arrived, accompanied by a local Inspector, I greeted them soberly but (I hope) sensibly, ushered them into the drawing-room and brought them coffee (they took it black). Inspector

Parkin I already knew, but the Superintendent I had not seen before. His name was Coulton, and he had been sent from Leeds. He was a man of about fifty—perhaps not over-imaginative, but with a face that was drawn, and either sad or tired. Not a man, I suspected, who had ever been particularly happy in his job, or one who had particularly enjoyed many of the things it had forced him to do. But no doubt he had done them. And however much I might have been disposed to like him in other circumstances, I was wary of him in these. Very wary.

He sat down on the sofa when I did, all of us very sober, and me rather tense, and he looked around the room, giving no sign on that impassive face of whether he approved of our taste in pictures or not. Both he and Parkin had notebooks, in which they made very occasional jottings. When both of them had had a sip or two of the coffee, Coulton started straight in.

'Mrs Kitterege,' he began, 'I believe you became aware of your husband's death—'

'When I saw him floating down the river,' I interrupted, in a metallic voice that surprised me. I lowered it. 'It's not a very nice way to learn you're a widow.'

'No. It must have been quite horrifying. When did you last see your husband?'

I had to suppress irrelevant associations with Victorian historical paintings.

'Just before I took my lunch-break. That was quite late. About two, or a bit later, I think. Mrs Nielson may remember more accurately. I'd been waiting for Mr Horsforth, whom I shared the junk stall with, to come back. When he did, I took off with Mrs Nielson, who had the jam stall opposite.'

'And did you talk to your husband outside, by the Test Your Strength machine, which I gather he ran?'

'No—he'd come in, and had been chatting with me by my stall. Colonel Weston was filling in outside, and Marcus said that he was hoping to go home for a longish break around three-thirty. I'm afraid when Mr Horsforth turned up, I just took off.' Tears welled up as I thought of the briskness of my last leave-taking of Marcus, but I suppressed them. 'I was afraid he'd disappear again, and we'd never get any lunch.'

'And you and Mrs Nielson were together the whole time during lunch?'

I tried not to tense up, or become obviously wary.

'No. We went to a corner of the meadow to eat our sandwiches. Then her dog demanded a proper walk, so she went off, and I just stayed there for a bit.'

'Alone?'

'Yes, alone . . . Though anyone could have seen me there. I didn't want to go back to the tent at once. I felt I'd rather been taken advantage of by Mr Horsforth.'

'But you did eventually go back. How long had you been alone in the meadows by then?'

'About fifteen minutes, I suppose. Quite long enough to murder my husband.'

The tired eyes raised themselves from the pad on which Coulton was making a note of those fifteen minutes. They looked at my flushed face, as if they had been through all this before.

'We don't know when your husband was murdered, Mrs Kitterege, but the indications are that it was decidedly later than the time we are talking about at the moment. We are just trying to get our picture of the whole afternoon straight. So—you will have got back to the tent when?'

'I really don't know. But somewhere about twenty to three, I imagine.'

'And you didn't talk to your husband outside the tent?'

'No. I didn't see him. Colonel Weston was running his game. Which is odd, because it was certainly nothing like three-thirty. Perhaps Marcus had gone to do something special—or just gone to the loo, perhaps.'

'I'll ask Colonel Weston. And did you leave your stall again before—before you went out and saw your husband's body?'

'No. I've thought it over. Mr Horsforth never came back to relieve me after my lunch-break.'

I felt like adding, 'So if you want to pin the murder of Marcus on me, you'll have to fix it much earlier than you thought.' I suppressed it, because I'd had one unwise outburst already; but the tired eyes were on me, and I suppose he recognized that we were both thinking along the same lines. I said:

'When do you think it happened?'

'We don't know. We are obviously going to have to do a lot of interviewing, testing of people's memories, because of course the medics won't be able to pinpoint it at all exactly. The trouble is, at a fête, people don't keep looking at their watches the whole time.'

'I did,' I said. 'But I suppose you don't if you're just attending and enjoying yourself. But what makes you say that you think the . . . the crucial time was later?'

The eyes sharpened as they looked at me.

'We've made no absolute decision about the likely time of death, you understand.' (Meaning, don't think you're off the hook, my girl.) 'And we haven't even begun to interview people systematically. But we have had one sighting of your husband volunteered, and that was quite a bit later than your lunch-break.'

'How much later?'

'Shortly after half past three. The witness says she saw your husband leaving the meadows, heading in the direction of the town square—presumably on his way home.'

'She?' I inquired.

'Yes.' He consulted his notes. 'A Miss Mary Morse.' A quick glance at Inspector Parkin showed that he'd been informed that Mary was one of the town busybodies.

'And did Miss Mary Morse claim to have exchanged

words with my husband?' I asked, unable to keep a barbed quality out of my voice. The Superintendent flicked back through his notebook.

'She claims that he said: "It's gone very well so far, hasn't it?" And that she replied: "Very well indeed."'

I reflected. Robbed of the undertow and the tones of voice, the conversation sounded innocuous. No wonder Mary reported it. But I couldn't rid myself of the idea that there must have been more to Mary's burst of public spirit than met the eye.

'At what time did Miss Morse come to you and volunteer this information?' I asked.

'At about nine-thirty last night.'

'Ah,' I said. 'And what *else* did she volunteer?'

Superintendent Coulton looked at me, quite sharply.

'Why do you think she volunteered anything else?'

'Because I snapped her head off on the phone shortly after nine. If she came along to you about nine-thirty, it will have been to get some sort of revenge, though I'm sure she told herself she was only doing her civic duty. Treat what she said with caution.'

'I treat all the information I get with caution,' said Superintendent Coulton, and though he was looking at me meaningfully as he said it, I thought it was probably true, and felt the better for it. Hexton was not easily going to put it over on him. He leaned back in his chair. 'Mrs Kitterege, were you happily married?'

He was telling me, quite informally, of the tendency of Mary Morse's other 'information'. My blood boiled, but I tried to answer as simply and directly as possible.

'Yes, we were. Very happily married. We loved each other very much.'

'Tell me what sort of a man your husband was.'

Well, you know how I saw Marcus. I talked about him for some time, telling the Superintendent the sort of things I would probably never have said about Marcus to his face.

In the sharpness of my sense of loss, I probably enthused about him, and perhaps this was unwise, perhaps almost suspicious. The Superintendent's eyes were hooded; the Inspector stopped taking notes (the character of the deceased was not 'fact', perhaps). After a few minutes I ground to a halt, and had to suppress a sob. The Superintendent repeated:

'And you were perfectly happily married?'

'Yes, I've said so.'

'You did not, either of you, go in for . . . extra-marital adventures?'

'We did not,' I said. 'Whatever Mary Morse may have said.'

'I would ask some such question of any wife whose husband had been murdered,' said Coulton.

'That must make you very popular with the recently bereaved. In this case, I suppose that Mary's little chat has ensured that you come here with your mind already made up,' I said, unable to suppress the bitterness I felt. 'Has the good Miss Morse also kindly supplied you with a name to pin these extra-marital activities on to?'

I saw what Mary had been trying to do: distract police attention from the major cause of strife in Hexton over the last few weeks—her own activities. On the other hand, I did wonder who Mary could have picked on for Marcus's covert love-life. It's not that there was any lack of attractive women in the country around Hexton, but in Hexton itself everyone for one reason or another had a faint air of unlikeliness about them. Mary must have had to think quickly to find anyone, and I wondered who on earth she had picked.

'You really mustn't put my questions down to Miss Morse, and I assure you that my mind is not made up.' The Superintendent had a good line in patience, giving me the impression that he might be the father of a brood of rather tiresome children. 'However, there has been one name mentioned. Tell me, how friendly was your husband with Lady Godetia Peabody?'

For the first time since Marcus's death I giggled, and the giggle swelled to a yelp of laughter. Mary really had been scraping the bottom of the barrel. When I recovered, I said:

'You may think that I was in the dark over Marcus's sexual habits, and I'm sure a lot of wives are. But I assure you I do know something about his tastes. You'll be wasting your time if you start investigating the possibility of an affair between Marcus and Lady Godetia.'

'She was heard to say he was "madly attractive".'

'I'm sure she did. I can imagine Lady Godetia saying that about almost anyone: Denis Thatcher, Ronald Reagan —anyone a degree or two more attractive than Yassir Arafat. Whether anyone would ever be attracted to her is another matter. *Are* there men who are turned on by that Anna Neagle manner?'

I could see our local Inspector Parkin was shocked. Widows did not make jokes of that kind—or perhaps he considered Anna Neagle sacrosanct. He marked me down, if he had not done so long ago, as a sharp-tongued bitch. Well, I had no complaint about that.

'We won't pursue that,' said Coulton, with a sigh.

'I bet you *do*. But you'll be wasting your time. You know what Mary's trying to do, don't you?'

'Well—' Superintendent Coulton threw a look at the Inspector.

'She's using anything to hand—and clutching rather desperately, I may say—to divert attention from her own recent activities.'

'Right. Then let's get on to them. Now first of all, tell me about your husband's position in the town.'

'His position? Well, as you must know, he's a vet. Was a vet. He served on the town council for a bit—just a couple of years.'

'Why not longer?'

'He was sort of squeezed out. There wasn't any room for Independents any longer. Party politics took over, and they all started calling themselves Conservatives. That's what Marcus was, but he drew the line at calling himself one. So most of his community activity these last few years has been through the Church.'

'Why the Church?'

'Why not?' I asked defensively. After all, even I had to admit that there was nothing either perverse or absurd about being a Christian. 'He's always been involved in the Church since he was a boy. He was one of the churchwardens at St Edward the Confessor's. Where, as I suspect you have already heard, there's been a lot of fur flying these last few months.'

'Yes, I had heard. And as an outsider I find it rather difficult to understand. What was your husband's position in it all?'

'His function was to smooth ruffled feathers. That was always Marcus's function. He would go around trying to convince people that they were making a lot of fuss about nothing. They were, but mostly he didn't convince them.'

'Among the ruffled feathers were Miss Mary Morse's?'

'Pre-eminent among them were Mary's. With Thyrza Primp's a good second. Thyrza is moving away, otherwise she would have been more active. When he failed to soothe, Marcus had reluctantly to take a stand—just as a matter of common sense and good manners, and it was then that he couldn't avoid rousing people against him. The bone of contention was Father Battersby, who is apparently too High Church for Mary and her gang, and celibate to boot. For some reason Mary conceives a vicar's wife to be the pivot and mainstay of the parish, though God knows the precedent of Thyrza Primp might make most people hope for a few years' respite from vicars' wives.'

This time, I noticed, my sharpness won a sympathetic grin from Inspector Parkin. Presumably he too had suffered.

'You don't like these women?' asked Superintendent Coulton, in one of those statements of the obvious that I suppose policemen are forced to go in for.

'I . . . don't . . . like . . . them . . . at . . . all,' I said, spacing it out venomously to make clear my sincerity.

'I see. I must say I still find it an area of controversy that I can't quite understand.'

'Read a few minor mid-Victorian novels and you'd understand it better. Hexton is a very mid-Victorian community, heavily diluted. And you have to remember that most of the people here are bored—sometimes out of their minds.'

'And as far as you are concerned, it is this business of the new vicar that's at the bottom of your husband's murder?'

I thought for a bit.

'Yes . . . Perhaps in some indirect way that we haven't yet understood. It all seems so trivial, but it has aroused very high feelings. And truly—you don't have to take my word for it, ask anyone—Marcus was such a peaceable, loving man, there just isn't any other reason I can think of. The trouble is that Colonel Weston, the senior church-warden, is rather a lethargic person, though well-meaning enough, so when all the fuss blew up, it was Marcus, inevitably, who found himself in the firing line.'

I stopped, appalled.

'I haven't asked you how he was killed. *Was* he shot?'

'No, he wasn't.' He looked at me closely. 'I notice you assume he wasn't simply drowned.'

'How could anyone drown Marcus?' I asked impatiently. 'He was very strong. It would take ages, and great strength and expertise, to hold him under. It just couldn't have happened in Hexton on fête day. There would be bound to be people come along.'

'He could have been stunned and thrown in,' Inspector Parkin pointed out.

'Yes . . . Funny, I never thought of that . . . But I suppose that's because I thought of him as on his way home—

walking busily along. Not standing by the river dreamily, asking to be hit from behind . . . But that wasn't how he was killed, was it?'

'No. He was dead when he went into the water. How long there was between his death and his being thrown in we don't yet have enough information to judge. The medics will pronounce on that eventually, I suppose, but I'm not expecting that they'll come up with anything very useful. There are some odd things about the body—dirt on the flesh and on the clothes that the river hadn't quite washed away, and some bruises—which we're going to have to account for. He could have fallen—'

'From Castle Walk!' I exclaimed.

'Why do you mention that?'

'It's the obvious place, isn't it? It towers over the meadows and the river. I never could work out why Marcus would be going home along the river. It's a very long way round, and he hadn't got much time for his cup of tea and his pipe. Castle Walk is longer than through the town square, but not by much, and it's a path he was very fond of. And of course it would be much cooler on a hot day.'

'Yes,' said Coulton. 'That would explain it.'

'And—' I hesitated, because this would be painful. Marcus had liked pain no more than most. 'How did he actually die?'

'He was stabbed to the heart with something very thin and sharp. It would certainly have been a very quick death. The blow was either a very lucky one, or a very knowledge-able one.'

'The weapon,' I said, forcing myself to keep my tone absolutely clinical, 'was withdrawn from the body?'

'Yes. We have little or no idea what it could have been. The very finest of stilettos—but even that would seem to be too crude. Anyone around here with connections with Italy or Spain? Seen anything like that in anybody's home—perhaps a war souvenir?'

I thought. One didn't like to think of the interiors of most of the houses in Hexton, but in the course of my getting together stuff for my stall I had recently seen the inside of a great number.

'People's houses here are full of such incredible bric-à-brac,' I said. 'Naturally I relied on that when I was collecting for the junk stall, though in fact I found they very seldom wanted to get rid of it, and resented it being described as bric-à-brac, let alone as junk. Thyrza Primp, to take an extreme case, was convinced that all the rubbish she loaded off on to me was stuff that anyone would find either useful of decorative, though I knew people wouldn't touch it with a bargepole . . . Italy . . . I know Colonel Weston was at Monte Cassino, and fought his way up to Venice. But I've never seen anything like a stiletto in his house. He's more a gun man—slaughtering wild life, and that sort of thing. The Culpeppers had a holiday in Amalfi a few years ago, but it doesn't sound as if your average tourist souvenir is the sort of thing you're looking for . . . Mary Morse and her mother made a pilgrimage to the Holy Land years ago. They felt the dirt was sanctified by the associations. They came back with all manner of hideous souvenirs, but I don't think Israel is famous for its delicate weapons, is it? . . . I really can't think . . . But you said that a stiletto—'

I was interrupted by the telephone.

'That's probably for me,' said Superintendent Coulton.

He strode over to the phone and said the number. Then he said 'Coulton here,' and stood there, listening for some minutes. I noticed an expression of satisfaction on his face. Then he snapped out 'I'll be right over,' and banged down the phone.

'Well, it looks as though we're one step ahead,' he said. 'We've got a lead on how the body got into the water.'

CHAPTER 8

OUR GALLANT BOYS

When the two policemen had gone, leaving me with no idea of what their new lead might be, I cleared away the coffee-cups, washed up the few odds and ends that were sitting around in the kitchen, and then went next door to fetch Jasper. He had been left there on the morning of the fête, and had been there, shamefully forgotten, ever since. His welcome to me was rapturous. Mrs Leadbury, who had been looking after him, was more awkward. She began: 'Oh, Mrs Kitterege, I *was* so shocked—' and then 'You don't *have* to take him, you know, I'd be only too happy—' But then she subsided into silence. Death is a great nonplusser.

I found that out again later. Jasper nosed his way about the house, and registered that Marcus was not home. But he was used to that, and in the end he settled down in one of 'his' corners of the house, fixing me with an expectant black eye. He thought it was his right to be taken for a walk.

I thought so too, as a matter of fact. And as I said before, I had no notion of conforming to Hexton's code of confinement for the recently widowed. Still, going out into the town—however much of a relief it would be to get it over—required some psychological preparation: it was a question of screwing one's courage to the sticking place. And then there was the question of where to go. In the end I decided that the best place to go was the most outrageous: I decided to take Jasper to the spot where I believed Marcus to have been murdered. I could imagine the commentary that would be lavished on *that* act over the next few days in Hexton.

The first thing I realized as I walked through town on the way to the castle was that Hexton's etiquette for widows was for the benefit of Hexton at large, and not for the benefit of the widows. Never since the day the Marquess of Queensberry had branded Oscar Wilde a 'somdomite' can there have been a public progress attended by so many abrupt about-turns or precipitate dives into shops. The fact that it was Sunday rendered the latter manœuvre particularly farcical and fruitless. Some people actually had to face me and greet me, their embarrassment patent and naked. At so hideous a spectacle as a widow walking her dog on the first morning of her widowhood, the burghers of Hexton suddenly seemed to see the advantages of the custom of Suttee.

The people I encountered were mostly the godless of Hexton, for the churches were not yet out. Heaven knows what paroxysms of outrage I would have met with if Mary, Thyrza and Co. had been on the streets. As it was, I gained the spot where the town gives way to the castle keep and Castle Walk itself without meeting any of those whom I particularly associated with the unhappiness and strife of Marcus's last days.

I stopped at that point, and gazed down into the valley and to the parish church of St Edward the Confessor. The cars parked around the church were surely more numerous than in the days when Walter Primp had preached of a safe, middle-of-the-road God, distinguishable from a dull, backbench Tory MP only by his omniscience? Yes, definitely there were more cars. I strained my eyes. That, surely, was the ancient Mercedes owned by Franchita and Howard Culpepper? As I watched, the clock in the town square struck twelve, and soon after people began to stream out. Yes—it had been a very large congregation indeed. Mary's God bus must have been all but empty, setting the seal on her humiliation. An emotion oddly compounded of pleasure and bitterness flooded over me. How delighted Marcus would have been. But did he need to have died to bring it about?

A sharp bark from Jasper brought my attention back. We turned away from the town and continued along Castle Walk. At the town end of the Walk the wooded slope down to the meadows is a comparatively gentle one. As you continue up and around the castle walls the slope becomes precipitous, and less heavily wooded, until just above the weir it is the sort of sheer drop that vertigo sufferers have great difficulty getting past. It was here that I had in mind for Marcus's fall, and as I rounded the bend that approached it, I realized that I was not alone in my idea. At that point along the walk a little knot of four or five policemen were collected.

As they saw me approach, one of them stepped forward to turn me away, thinking I was one of the sensation-seekers they had probably already had their fill of. Another one, who knew me, put his hand on his arm and whispered in his ear. When I came nearer, this second one came up to me and said:

'Are you sure you want to be here, Mrs Kitterege?'

I nodded, and went ahead to the spot at which they were standing. It was difficult to know quite what made one so sure that this was the place where Marcus had gone down. Just a matter of a few broken stalks, a sparse, precarious bush that seemed to have been knocked sideways, grass flattened that had not yet righted itself; yet somehow these meagre indications added up to a trail, from the most precipitous section of Castle Walk, down to the path beside the weir.

'Yes,' I said. 'I think it must have been here.'

The policemen didn't know quite what to say. Most of them I knew, or had talked to, because Marcus's work brought him quite often into contact with the police, due to strays, quarantine regulations, or cattle thefts. They were awkward with me, but used to me, and soon one of them, a sensible young man, began pointing out the indications, one after another, of Marcus's path down, coolly, as if he were giving a demonstration at Police College. It was bracing, and well done, but I noticed he kept his hand on my arm the whole time, as we stood at the edge of that dizzying drop. Finally I thanked him, and continued my way round the castle.

The path led me, eventually, back into town, and to a point not very far from the police station. Once again people —friends, even—made the most obvious manœuvres to avoid coming face to face with me, but I ploughed grimly on: they were going to have to get used to it. I too, for that matter, was going to have to get used to it. On an impulse, not quite knowing what I was going to do when I got inside, I turned into the police station.

There was a desk sergeant on duty, and some young men sitting around the walls. Somewhat abruptly, to cover my embarrassment, I said to the desk sergeant:

'The Superintendent was called away during our talk. I wondered if he was free now.'

'That's right: it was me that called him. I'll see if he can talk to you now. May I say how sorry I am, Mrs Kitterege? We thought the world of your husband in our family. He treated my little girl's hamster last year, and he couldn't have gone to more trouble if it'd been a prize racehorse.'

My heart went out to the man. It was possible to do the right thing in a simple and graceful manner.

'Thank you. That's the nicest thing anyone has said to me. Marcus never made any distinctions.'

'I expect you can guess what the Super's up to,' whispered the sergeant as he left, jerking his head towards the young men lining the walls. I looked at them properly for the first time.

They were, not to put too fine a point on it, an ill-favoured bunch. One was long and thin, his shanks so spindly and covered with such close-fitting jeans that one could imagine a tailor sewing them around matchsticks. Another was pudgy and blotchy, his arms and even his neck hideously and obscenely tattooed. All of them were sweaty and surly, and gave off a stale odour of hangovers and long-term personal neglect.

Suddenly I realized who they must be: these were 'our gallant boys'—ones from the lower end of the acceptability scale. They were also, I strongly suspected, the more unpleasant of the two drunken parties at the fête. My stomach gave a slight heave as I realized why they must be here.

'The Superintendent suggests you go in,' said the desk sergeant, coming back softly behind me. He led me through to a bare, draughty interviewing room, where Superintendent Coulton sat behind a desk, and where another version of the boys outside sat on an uncomfortable-looking wicker chair. He was well-built, but too fleshy to be impressive, and the tattoos on his arm and the four or five ripe boils on his face added to the feeling that he was pathetic rather than dangerous, however truculent his air.

'This is Mrs Kitterege,' said Coulton gloomily. 'It was her husband you tipped into the river.'

'I didn't mean no harm,' protested the boy, his voice having overtones of whine which robbed it of menace. He looked at the sneakers he wore, never at me. 'It were just a bit o' fun. I were that pissed.'

'Perhaps you'd like to go over, for Mrs Kitterege's benefit, exactly what happened,' said Superintendent Coulton.

The boy grimaced. 'I've bin through it.'

'Again.'

The boy sighed, exaggeratedly. The world was being hard on him—for no reason, no reason at all.

'Well, there was this bloke—big bloke in a green jacket—'e coom down to us by t'river, an' 'e told us to stop spoiling other people's fun, that's 'ow 'e put it. 'E 'ad no call to say that. We weren't doin' nowt.'

'That was about a quarter to three,' supplied Coulton

under his breath. 'I think that's why your husband wasn't at the games when you went back to the tent.'

'So we didn't want no trouble, an' it weren't much fun at the bleedin' fête, so we just took up us bags—we 'ad a few more cans in them—and went away. We sat us down by t'river for a while, and had us each a can, an' larked about a bit. Just fun. You've got to let off steam once in a while. Then another lot of army lads coom up from t'fête. We shouted at 'em a bit—a slangin' match, like—and we went on up t'road along by t'river and up to t'weir. That was when we saw it, like.'

'The body?'

'Aye.'

'Where was it exactly?'

'Nearly at t'weir, but on t'other side of t'path, face down. An' I said: "Here, that's that stupid prick that bawled us out." An' someone said: "'E's dead drunk." 'Cos we was dead pissed, like, an' we didn't think. An' I said: "Chook 'im into t'river to sober 'im up." I didn't mean no 'arm. I meant to go in after an' get 'im out, honest I did, once 'e'd 'ad a soakin'.' He looked up momentarily, saw that he was not being believed, and looked down to his jogging shoes again. 'So we got 'old of 'im, two on us, an' dragged 'im across the path, an' chucked 'im in. Then, as us watches 'im, I looks down an' sees there's blood on me 'ands, an' I knew it weren't mine. I said: "He were dead!" an' we all scarpered . . . It were awful . . . Like we'd done it, some'ow.'

He went silent for a minute, and it was obvious that this was a moment of horror that had actually got through his thick skull.

'One of t'other lot—the lads as was be'ind us—tried to wade in an' get 'im out, but t'current were too strong. 'E'd got caught up in a bloody great branch. But they told on us when we got back to barracks . . . Stupid gits . . . We'll get even wi' 'em.'

'I don't think you will, you know,' said Coulton. 'Well,

Mrs Kitterege, I'm afraid that's the story of how your husband came to be in the river.'

I sat down for a moment on another little hard chair. It was stupid to be sentimental about what happened to a body, but these thick-headed, brutal louts seemed to add one further outrage to the monstrous outrage that had already been inflicted on it. Momentarily I felt sick, but I swallowed and was all right.

'Yes,' I said at last. 'Thank you for letting me hear his story. Now all we have to find out is how it came to be there by the weir.'

When I left the Superintendent he was deciding what to do with these unprepossessing specimens of the soldiery. I said I thought they might be left to the military authorities. They were marginal—'nasty but marginal,' I said—and the Superintendent seemed to agree.

I had intended to go straight home, and Jasper, in spite of his irritation at the interruptions to his walk, seemed willing. But as I walked, grim-faced and not encouraging converse (even had anyone been willing to offer it), a whole host of things were buzzing around in the back of my mind, yet refusing to form themselves into any recognizable shape or pattern that could enable me to say that I had come some steps further. It was mainly the desire to talk things over with a sympathetic soul that determined me, when I passed her house, to call on Mrs Nielson. She lived, as we did, somewhat on the outskirts of Hexton. The prized houses in the town are the old stone ones, built directly on to the wynds. They are quaint but poky, and not all of them even have a back garden. They would never have done for a vet's surgery, and so we have a largeish, late-Victorian house ten minutes from the centre, with Simon Fox, Marcus's partner, living three doors down. Mrs Nielson had a much smaller house, between us and town, but she had ample garden both back and front, which was already showing vigorous signs of her activity during this her first spring in the house. As I went up the front drive I heard her through the open front door talking to Gustave:

'*There's* a clever boy, then . . . Now a little more . . . My precious has got to eat, hasn't he? . . . Just one more bit of the nice chicken, and then we'll go walkies . . .'

Jasper sniffed as I rang the doorbell. Poodles might like being talked to in this manner, he seemed to imply, but a rangy mongrel like himself would sooner die.

'Helen!'

As soon as she saw me, Gwen Nielson buried her head on my shoulder, drew me inside, and together we had a good, short weep. I knew she was a sensible woman. It was what I had been needing all day, though it was not something I would want to have done with many of the women in Hexton. She led me through into the living-room, where the Victorian contours of the room did not seem to conflict at all with the clean-lined Scandinavian furniture.

'Such a lovely man,' she said. 'I can't tell you how I liked him. I just can't take it in. It all seems so . . . so damned *random*.'

The dogs were setting up a great racket, Gustave with his high-speed soprano barking, Jasper with a playful snapping at his haunches. 'Out!' said Gwen Nielson, and bundled them unceremoniously out into the garden.

'He's off-colour,' she said, talking of Gustave. 'Probably something from that damned sandwich stand yesterday. Now I shall never again have Marcus to take him to . . . Come along and sit down. I suppose that what you really want is a talk.'

'Yes,' I said. 'I do . . . But I suppose what I really want is to find out who killed Marcus.'

'I see,' said Gwen. 'But is there anything you can do that the police won't do equally well, or better? Is it that you don't trust the man in charge?'

'No—it's not that. I do trust him. He seems quiet and

thorough. He doesn't seem to suspect me any more than he's bound to. Since I gather the majority of murders *are* domestic murders, then he's probably only doing what statistics have laid down for his guidance . . . I know I'm sounding childish, but in fact I think I really want to do a bit of nosing around because I need something to do. Something to take me out of the emptiness of the house, the emptiness all around me.'

'I know. That's how all widows feel. It's perfectly normal.'

'By Hexton's Victorian standards I ought to be prostrate. Overcome with the vapours and attended by some soft-footed medical practitioner who specializes in "women's ailments". Well, I'm damned well not going to be prostrate for them.'

'Good for you. On the other hand, I still don't see exactly what you can do.'

'There is one advantage I have over the Superintendent: I know Hexton. I know it both as an outsider and an insider. I know the class divisions, I know the divide between church and chapel, I know the tensions between the locals and those of us who've moved here for one reason or another. And above all, I know the women . . . What did you call it? The town of the witches.'

Mrs Nielson blushed.

'Don't remind me. What an appalling *faux pas*. But I think that's an important point: a policeman would never really understand the women here, would never get to the bottom of the world they live in. To me, coming from outside, it seemed staggering—the pettiness of their lives and concerns. It's from another century.'

'It's the women who rule in Hexton,' I said, repeating what I had said so long ago to Marcus. 'Petty they may be, but they have the whip hand, and they enjoy it. And it's somewhere there that the key lies . . . The difficulty will be in getting started. At the moment everyone seems to dive down manholes, rather than meet me face to face.'

'I'm afraid you're probably going right against Hexton etiquette in going out at all.'

'Oh, I am. I'm quite aware of that.'

'On the other hand, I seem to remember at the time when Mary Morse's mother died . . . don't they make *calls*?' She spoke as if she were discussing the beings of another planet, dropping in on us in UFOs. 'I didn't, of course, on Mary, because I was too new then, and didn't know her well. And anyway, I couldn't quite believe that people still did such things. But they did! I remember a long procession of people went, one by one, calling on her—at tea-time, or morning coffee-time, or whatever.'

'You're right, of course. That's what people do here.'

'In that case, won't they call on you? And won't that give you your opportunity?'

'I *suppose* they will call on me. Even though I try to be as little Hexton as possible. They'll do it because of Marcus's position—a vet is rather important in a town full of ageing people with horrible animals . . . Sorry, I wasn't referring to you or Gustave . . . So I suppose they will, though it's always possible that some special rule applies when murder is in question . . . I don't think I'll risk it. I always did like turning Hexton customs on their heads. I think I shall cause great scandal. I shall pay *my* mourning calls on *them*.'

CHAPTER 9

CASTLE WALLS

I spent the first part of the next day in thought. So did Jasper. He moped. Marcus, he thought, was away, as he occasionally was, to conferences, or on a difficult case at some remote farm. Jasper, I feared, was going to mope still more before the week was out, and, with that blessed shortness of canine memory, he began to forget. I, meanwhile, had not the heart to attempt any of those tactics for cheering him up which I usually employed to keep his mind off Marcus's absences.

I was thinking. First of all I was wondering whether I dared to pay the first of my mourning calls that day. There were limits to my daring in defiance of Hexton custom—I was a Fabian rather than a revolutionary by temperament. Also, my embarrassed reception of the day before had made me wary. But, more than that, I was uncertain how I was to approach the crux of the matter on these visits. 'Where were you when my husband was killed?' spoken above the tinkle of teaspoons on bone china, seemed a preposterous intrusion, and one likely to get me nowhere at all. I could not even explain why I believed that the murderer of Marcus was to be found among the middle-class residents of Hexton whose quarrels he had spent his last days trying to dampen down. Hexton, I had no doubt, had by now fixed on one of the army boys, or perhaps all of them, as culprit. Rumour would swiftly have broadcast their inquisition by the Superintendent, and Hexton would have breathed a relieved (and self-congratulatory) sigh: it was the sort of thing they had more or less expected. 'I always said that *one day* . . .' they would be saying to one another.

But they were wrong, wilfully wrong. They were setting up a smoke-screen. It was they who had killed Marcus. One of them. The question was: how to manage the discussions that eventually might give me a lead as to which of them it was. I began to think that aggression, blatancy, was my only possible form of approach.

After lunch—I was eating ravenously still—I made a concession to weakness and pain and had a lie-down. As the afternoon wore on, and I still had made no decision and lighted on no definite plan of campaign, it became imperative to take Jasper for his daily walk. Moping or not, he was a dog who kept his mind—and mine—on his few and simple needs. He perked up no end when he heard the jingle of his lead. Impelled by I-knew-not-what, we made once more in the direction of the castle.

As I neared the place where Castle Walk began, and the little cluster of cottages around the entrance to the castle itself, I thought I had an inkling of why I had been drawn in this direction again. Castle Walk was largely shielded from the meadows, and from the lower paths along the river and past the weir, by its height and by the vegetation on its slopes. On the other hand, it went *around* the castle—that is, *beneath* its walls. How far, then, was the Walk visible from the grounds inside the castle walls? Hexton Castle was not a particularly popular tourist spot, but there are always castle buffs, and one or two of all the tourists who would be in Hexton on a Saturday in summer would be sure to feel that they had to see what there was to be seen. So tourists there would have been, around the castle somewhere, at the time when Marcus was stuck to the heart.

I turned away from the Walk, and made my way up the sloped, cobbled path leading to the castle gate.

'You can't take that dog in with you,' said a bossy little functionary in blue. I knew that perfectly well, but in the stress of the moment had forgotten.

'Why on earth not?' I asked, preparing to argue the toss.

'It's a national monument. No dogs. *Nor* in the approaches. You'll have to tie him up down there.'

'Really, that's quite nonsensical,' I complained, approaching him. 'What harm can dogs do? It's human beings who damage national monuments.'

'They bark, and the people around complain.' That figured. They would. Hexton divided itself up very neatly into the doggy and the anti-dog people. I sometimes thought we should have some sort of Group Areas Act, to divide us from each other, and laws against intermarriage. The bossy little man was by now looking at me closely. 'It's Mrs Kitterege, isn't it? Oh dear, oh dear,' he fussed. 'Well, I suppose we *might* make an exception ... in the circumstances. But keep him on his lead!'

I shot him a look that was not composed mainly of gratitude, paid my money, and walked through the gateway, set in the wall by the keep. As I walked on I knew he would have popped into the ticket-office to nudge, stare and comment. He was that sort of little man.

My first task was to ascend to the parts of the keep open to visitors, and ascertain what could be seen from there. That was easily done. Magnificent views, but nothing of Castle Walk, which clutched to the base of the high castle walls. Almost certainly, then, if anything were seen, it would have to have been from the trimmed, grassy expanses of the Great Court, for the various ruined rooms and chapels around the Court had only slit windows, through which it was impossible to put one's head. The lawns of the Great Court, on the other hand, stretched to the top of the castle's walls, and visitors often sunbaked, picnicked or larked about on them.

I walked somewhat gingerly to the far end of the Court. I am not afraid of heights, but Jasper is inclined to give sudden jerks on his lead if he sees anything that interests him. From here one got an excellent view of Castle Walk, on its first stretch from the town, but lost it as the path curved round towards the precipitous slope down to the weir, down which Marcus had fallen or been pushed. I walked carefully round the walls, as close to the edge as I could manage: at the crucial stage, the view of the path was blocked by the ruined wall of a battery. I was not surprised, or too disappointed: people who witnessed murders were inclined to report what they had seen to the police. If anyone had seen anything from the castle walls which they had not yet gone to the police with, it would have to be something they had seen *before* the murder—something that they had not yet realized the significance of ... Marcus walking, Marcus meeting up with someone ... I returned to the point on the walls from which one got a good view of Castle Walk, and sat down with Jasper, thinking and observing.

Castle Walk was an excellent place for a stroll, for it was seldom crowded: Hexton was a small town, and the tourists tended to cling to the centre. Thus, what one saw was *occasional* people walking past. And thus, even on a Saturday, Marcus could be murdered, his body fall fifty feet, and nothing be observed. As I sat there, in the late afternoon sun, watching, I saw people that I knew, going past one by one: Mrs Hussein from the delicatessen, wheeling her youngest child in a push-chair; one of the Blatchley children; a woman who cleaned for Thyrza Primp; Timothy and Fiona . . .

There was something odd about Timothy and Fiona. Well, there always was, in my opinion, but particularly today. Timothy, I knew, was on holiday from the firm of accountants where he worked; Fiona was pretty much perpetually on holiday. They came from town, holding hands, and gazing dewily into each other's eyes. Timothy looked ahead, and coming round the curve was a teacher from Mr Horsforth's school, one of my occasional colleagues. Timothy and Fiona sauntered on, exuding young love like an aerosol spray. As the teacher passed them, they greeted him sweetly and respectfully, then went on gazing at each other, raptly. As his footsteps receded into the distance, however, and with no one else visible along the walk, they dropped their clasped hands, moved a pace away from one another, and seemed to retreat into separate worlds, Timothy gazing intently over at the distant landscape, Fiona brooding darkly as she kicked stones into the undergrowth at the side of the path. They were not hostile, merely separate. Only as they approached the curve did a glance pass between them—much like dancers, well-versed in their routine—whereupon Timothy's hand came out for Fiona's, they moved closer, and then walked towards the bend in the path for all the world like two amateur actors in the wings, about to make an entrance before all their friends and neighbours in the village hall.

'What a performance!' said a dark, slightly sardonic voice a few feet from me. I turned and saw Father Battersby.

He was standing a little behind me on the lawn, his black soutane billowing around his ankles in the light breeze, his lean, long, serious face looking concerned. His aspect was impressive, but slightly less 'other' than he had hitherto seemed to me. He had come to talk to me about Marcus, that I was sure, and I didn't yet know whether I wanted to or not. I looked back to the path, where Timothy and Fiona were disappearing around the bend, taking their dewy freshness towards the murder spot.

'Do you think so?' I asked.

'It must be. Young people may feel the same way about each other as they felt fifty, a hundred years ago, but they don't express it in the same way. Neither of those two has the strength of mind or originality to start a new trend, though there's something distinctly rum about that young man.'

'He certainly does seem too Leslie Howard for words.'

'I certainly won't be asking him to run the Lads' Brigade, anyway. But it wasn't those two I came to talk to you about, Helen.'

'I rather hoped you were just doing a tour of inspection of your new parish.'

'I was, until I saw you here. As a matter of fact, I was escaping from the Blatchley children. Everyone in that house is very kind, but of course they don't realize how exhausting children can be to an ageing bachelor.' He sat down on the grass, patted Jasper, who was beginning to give signs that this was not what he came out for, and looked at me concernedly. 'From what you say, I gather that you don't want to talk about your husband?'

I considered for a while.

'I shall eventually want to talk about him—and about *it*, to make sense of it in some way. Oh, don't worry: I'm not one of the sort of nutter who sees the fire in York Minster as God's divine thunderbolt punishing heresy, and I don't see any divine intervention in Marcus's death. I'm not going to lose my faith, such as it is, because I don't understand God's purpose in this. He doesn't have one, and this is a normal, messy, human affair. That's the trouble. Until I've reduced it to some kind of order in my mind, I can't focus on Marcus—on *himself*—as I want to. His end, and the randomness of it, keep getting in the way. So until the police find out who did it—'

'Or until you do—'

I looked up at him sharply.

'You've been talking to somebody.'

'Mrs Nielson did mention that you hoped to go around talking to people, perhaps getting to hear things that a Superintendent from Leeds is unlikely to be told.'

I sighed.

'However you put it, it sounds horribly Enid Blyton, doesn't it? I ought to be ashamed—'

'Not at all. My experience suggests that *any* activity is beneficial after a sudden loss—and yours was more horribly sudden than most. And of course you do know things about Hexton—the web of customs and conventions, the alliances and animosities—that the police could take months to get any real grasp of. I don't think there is anything *childish* as such in what you propose to do. Only, be careful—'

'Because she may strike again? I've thought of that. I'll be on my guard.'

'How can you be on your guard when you've already assumed it's a woman?'

He sounded quite exasperated by my silliness, and he did have a point. It was hardly prudent to have wiped fifty per cent of the population clean of suspicion. Father Battersby sat thinking for a moment, and then said:

'Tell me, have you come to the conclusion that this was a planned murder?'

This I had thought out.

'I think it's possible. It would be easy enough to persuade Marcus to go round Castle Walk. It was one of his favourite spots. He told me that he was finishing his stint on the Test Your Strength machine at three-thirty, so he could have told anyone, or anyone could have overheard. Easy enough to intercept him on his way home.'

'Quite. And yet . . . You know, I incline to think this was a quite off-the-cuff affair.'

'Do people murder off the cuff?'

'I put it badly. I mean the result of a sudden impulse. After all, if it was planned, then it was a terribly dangerous and chancy murder, wasn't it? Let us grant that the murderer had gone over this castle thoroughly, to make sure that stretch of the path was not visible from any part of it. But that committed him *to* that part, and only that part. Then there are the fields on the other side of the river: that part of Castle Walk is not thickly vegetated, so someone with good eyesight might easily have seen something from the fields. How could he or she be sure no one would be in view on the path? What would he have done if someone had been? Planned, it seems so unlikely. On an impulse, it seems credible.'

'What could arouse anyone to such an impulse against Marcus? The least impulsive of men himself . . .?'

'Something he said, in a quarrel . . .'

'Marcus hardly ever quarrelled in his life. He had used up a ten-year ration of harsh words in the weeks before you arrived. On the other hand a feeling, welling up, of humiliation and failure . . . after your reception at the fête . . .'

'You've made up your mind that that was the motive, haven't you?'

Again, he was obviously trying to stop me committing myself to one notion.

'I think it must have something to do with it. Of course,

I realize you won't like members of your flock being suspected.'

'Come, come. I know as well as any that Christians can commit murder. Quite apart from anything else, I've been a jail chaplain. I'm only trying to tell you that you shouldn't settle on a motive, commit yourself to it, too early. I'm sure the police haven't.'

'Where were you,' I asked, out of the blue, for why, after all, should anyone suspect Father Battersby, 'when Marcus was killed?'

Father Battersby said cautiously: 'I'm not sure that I know exactly when Marcus was killed.'

'Let's say he left the meadows around half past three, or five or ten minutes after that. That would give us some time between a quarter to four and four o'clock for his arrival at that point on Castle Walk.'

Father Battersby sat, his chin in his cupped hand, his robe spread out around him, like a ballerina in mourning.

'From the point of view of an alibi, it's the later the better for me. I saw the Blatchleys going across the meadows on their way home, and I joined them. When we got home it was ten past four, because we commented that it had been a long day. So I was probably with them from about five to four. But before that—well, I suppose I was around and about, as I had been all day.'

'Enjoying your triumph,' I said, and it was not difficult for him to catch the note of bitterness in my voice.

'Truly I didn't regard it in that light. Nor, I may say, did Marcus.'

'No, I'm sorry. I never did live up to Marcus's standards, and even after his death I can't. But it's worth remembering that it's not how you two regarded it that's important. As far as other people were concerned, you had had—how shall I put it?—an exceptionally successful day. I gather Marcus said something of the sort to Mary Morse, on his way out from the fête.'

'Really?' His eyebrows went up.

'In some tactful and generalized form. Tell me, is it your impression that Mary Morse was still at the fête when you left? I ask because you were one who had a great number of opportunities of observing her.'

'She did rather put herself in my way . . . My impression is that none of those encounters occurred later than, say, three or three-fifteen. But that's an impression only. Similarly, my predecessor's lady wife—who, by the way, is departing rather earlier than planned—wasn't greatly in evidence in the later part of the afternoon.'

'And why,' I asked sharply, 'is Thyrza Primp departing early for the gaieties of Harrogate?'

'I should have thought that there was one obvious explanation. You may not have heard, but she and Mary Morse were alone on their—' he smiled deprecatingly—'God bus yesterday. It can hardly have been a happy experience for her.'

'That's one explanation. I can think of others. I shall have to pay my call on her as soon as possible.'

At this point, though Father Battersby was talking, was most probably giving me words of advice or remonstration, my attention was drawn back to Castle Walk. The breeze that had fluttered the hem of his soutane when we started the conversation had risen to a real wind by now, and real winds make themselves felt on Castle Walk. Coming round the bend, from the point where Marcus had been killed (*how* people managed casually to pass by there, it seemed!) and heading towards town, was Mrs Mipchin. The wind drove her drab linen dress to cling immodestly around her legs and thighs, and tore at the scarf around her neck, and the pale grey felt hat on her head. As I watched, it nearly took the hat away, and Mrs Mipchin clutched at it, then drew from it a pin, and held both hat and pin in the safety of her hands.

'So, I repeat: take care,' Father Battersby concluded. 'Avoid making assumptions, don't act on them if you do.'

I looked around, but already he was striding away towards the gateway, over the trim lawns, his soutane billowing and giving him the air of a restless but purposive blackbird, flapping his way from crust to crust. I felt towards him warmly, yet he made me uneasy.

I turned back to Castle Walk and Mrs Mipchin, making her way grimly towards town. Clutched in her right hand, mesmerizing me, was that long, steel hatpin—a pin much like those that I had sold in such numbers on the day of the fête.

CHAPTER 10

CHEZ MIPCHIN

As Father Battersby disappeared through the gatehouse, I scrambled to my feet. Jasper barked his approbation, for the walk had not so far turned out at all as he had hoped. This earned us a frown from the bossy functionary as we hurried out into the wynds again. With a bit of luck Mrs Mipchin would be on her way home, and would pass by the cottages just below the castle. Jasper and I hurried ahead to meet her.

Her expression, as she saw us tripping down the steps, stumbling in our eagerness, was rather along the lines of Macbeth when he sees there is no empty seat at the feast. I, and Jasper, seemed to embody all that she most feared to encounter. I was not foolish enough to put this down to feelings of guilt: what she feared, most probably, was a social contretemps, a situation which no rules of behaviour had taught her how to cope with. It was rather like the Queen waking up to find a wild-eyed Irishman in her bedroom, but, if report be true, handled with considerably less aplomb.

'Oh, Mrs Kitt—Helen . . . This *is* surprising.'

'Hardly,' I said drily. 'I imagine Hexton has been buzzing with my flouting of its rules and conventions over the past day or two. I've met with nothing but embarrassment and avoidance every time I've put my nose outside my door.'

'I've always said,' Elspeth Mipchin enunciated, with that infuriating Edinburgh primness, 'that if we look behind what we call rules, we'll see that there is usually sound sense about human nature at the bottom of them.'

'Have you?' I said, with flat scorn in my tones. She had that sort of thin, genteel voice that often reads the serials on *Woman's Hour*. Her dreary complacency irritated me no end. 'The trouble is that people differ.'

'Ye-e-es,' she agreed. (How much better, it was implied, if they had not been so wilful as to do so, if they had all modelled themselves on the impeccable Elspeth Mipchin.)

'And I've already come to the conclusion that these rules are designed to spare people at large, not to help the bereaved.' Mrs Mipchin was not so stupid that she did not register that I was including her in a collective charge of hypocrisy and selfishness. I pressed home the advantage by saying: 'I was thinking of flouting the rules still more dramatically by asking you for a cup of tea.'

'Oh yes—of course—naturally.' Mrs Mipchin's house was only two minutes away, while mine was on the outskirts, and it seemed to be impossible to refuse, if only on humanitarian grounds. I did not want to leave her with the impression, however, that in my enfeebled and widowed state I had been exhausted by the afternoon sun. I said:

'I realize it should be *you* calling on *me*, but as you know I'm a perverse creature, and I don't know how long I'm going to be in Hexton to receive calls.'

Mrs Mipchin shot me a glance—composed of I know not what—as we walked through the narrow wynds.

'You are thinking of leaving Hexton?'

'As soon as I know who killed my husband,' I said calmly.

When we got to the Mipchins' front door—they lived in one of the stone houses that opened directly on to the wynds —Elspeth Mipchin looked pointedly at Jasper. Then we made our way without a word round to the back, and she waited while I tied him to the line post—neither asking nor suggesting that I do that, but taking it for granted that I knew that no dog was allowed to pollute the Mipchin interior with hairs, boisterousness or smell. Jasper spotted a King Charles bitch in the next garden, and seemed quite happy. Then Mrs Mipchin led me round again to the front door. To go in through the kitchen was unthinkable.

As we came through the door I thought I heard the sound of a television being switched off. Mrs Mipchin's ears also seemed to twitch suspiciously. She put her hat—the hatpin reinserted—into the hall cupboard and marched into the living-room.

'Mrs Kitterege has called for tea,' she announced, the ice of disapproval quite undisguised. The Mipchin residence was furnished with heavy and dark pieces of a kind that is rather unfairly called 'traditional'. It all sat squarely on the floor and announced 'I was not cheap.' Mr Mipchin was sitting over a coffee-table on which was a half-finished jigsaw puzzle, apparently of a vast cornfield in Upper Silesia. It looked very difficult, which was just as well, because I suspected it was just a blind to cover telly-watching when his wife was out of the way.

Elspeth Mipchin announced: 'I'll get the tea.'

That was a departure. George Mipchin was generally ordered to make the tea, while Elspeth saw to the dainties (who rated walnut sponge, and who could be fobbed off with lemon fingers being matters that demanded the nicest discrimination). Now she was undertaking both, no doubt intending to take her time, and leaving the hapless George to break the social ice. He did his duty well, if fussily, and ushered me into a chair by the empty grate.

'So you're getting about a bit again? Not shutting yourself away? That's right . . . That's good.'

'I find it helps, seeing people,' I said. 'Besides, I don't know how long I will be staying in Hexton, and I want to get things . . . sorted out.'

'You're thinking of leaving?' He sounded genuinely concerned. 'How sad. Where to?'

I hadn't really thought. Back to Mother? We would sit around the house both heartily wishing we were on our own. The whole thing was as yet more an idea than an intention, and the best thing about it was its usefulness as a catalyst.

'I don't know. I haven't decided. It will depend a bit on how I stand financially. Not Harrogate, anyway.'

George Mipchin shot me a sly smile. I added:

'I think the main thing is to get away from the town that killed my husband.'

I added that, I think, because Elspeth Mipchin was coming in with a tray of bone china, with a design of pink cornflowers on it. She looked aghast at my directness.

'What an extraordinary thing to say. If it were not for your . . . circumstances, I would use a stronger word. Everyone knows that your poor husband was killed by one or other of those drunken soldiers. I've always said that *one day*—'

'If everyone knows that,' I interrupted, 'they know a great deal more than Superintendent Coulton knows. I believe it's true that he has handed one of the soldiers over to the Military Police, but there's no question of a charge of murder.'

'But why not? The man is clearly not doing his duty!'

'The Superintendent rang me earlier today. Marcus was definitely stabbed on Castle Walk. Perhaps you saw the spot when you walked around it just now. It's becoming quite a tourist attraction, isn't it? This is quite certain, because his blood was found on grass and leaves on the slope. The soldiers were on the lower path by the weir—everyone is agreed on that. Unless they could be in two places at once, none of them could have murdered Marcus.'

Elspeth Mipchin stood there motionless, her mouth pursed up into her near-habitual expression of distaste. Then she turned without a word and returned to the kitchen.

'Ah!' said George Mipchin. '*Not* the soldier lads, then. That's a . . . pity.' I had the odd notion that his eyes were looking at me mischievously from *under* his Crippen moustache. 'I have the impression that people were rather clinging to that.'

'I've no doubt they were,' I said. 'When did you hear about the soldiers?'

'Someone—Mrs Culpepper would it be?—phoned Elspeth after church to say all those boys were at the police station. She said it had been much discussed after the service.'

'I can imagine. And thanks given during it by those who knew, I suppose. You were not at the service?'

'No . . . No . . . We discussed—*Elspeth* discussed—but in the end we didn't . . .'

'But you were not on the God bus?'

'No. No.' A little snigger burrowed its way through the moustaches. 'I believe the two good ladies who organized it were in fact alone on the bus. Again, we discussed whether we should go on it, as we had planned, but Elspeth decided—'

'*We* decided,' said Elspeth Mipchin, returning with a tray of eatables.

'Quite, my dear. When I say that you decided I mean that we decided.' He rolled an eye comically in my direction. 'After thinking things over, we came to the conclusion that it would be wisest to stay away altogether.

'It was a real spiritual struggle,' said Mrs Mipchin.

'It must have been,' I agreed. 'And in the end you decided to do nothing.'

'We watched the service on television,' said Elspeth

Mipchin defensively. 'Little though I approve of having it on in the daytime. A very pleasant service it was too. I have to admit we felt happier committing ourselves neither way.'

'And will you take your seat on Mary's bus next Sunday?'

Mrs Mipchin gave every sign of feeling boxed into a corner.

'Well, dear, we'll have to see, won't we? See how things go.'

What precisely, I wondered, did she mean by that? Elspeth Mipchin was not by nature a fence-sitter. What was going to bring her down on one side or the other? Did she mean that if, by next Sunday, Mary Morse or Thyrza Primp had not been arrested for murder, and what is more, if somebody had been, and for a motive that had nothing to do with all the ecclesiastical shenanigans, *then* Mrs Mipchin would consider putting her faith on the line and getting on the God bus, since it would have been disinfected of any questionable associations? I rather felt she did mean something like that. Such an interpretation did have the true, Victorian, Podsnappian ring to it.

Elspeth Mipchin had by now sat down, and was dispensing tea. The eatables, I noted, were a plate of Marie biscuits and another of quite unpleasant-looking sponge-fingers. Elspeth was trying to tell me something, I felt. I took one, and munched into it with a slightly exaggerated pantomime of enjoyment. I was tempted to say brightly, 'Did you enjoy the fête?' but that seemed unduly reminiscent of the mythical question supposed to have been put to Mrs Lincoln, so I merely said:

'Did you buy much at the fête?'

Mrs Mipchin shot me a suspicious glance. My words earlier had alerted her to my intention of finding out who had killed Marcus, but she could think of no valid reason for refusing to answer.

'Oh—some embroidered doylies . . . and some chutney

. . . some rather good early strawberries . . . And George bought something from your stall.'

'I remember,' I said. 'A doll in Welsh national costume, wasn't it? And did you buy anything from my stall?' I added, turning to Elspeth Mipchin.

'Nothing to speak of. Since George had bought something to remember poor dear Thyrza by . . .'

'Nothing to speak of. But suppose we do speak of it. Perhaps I could make a guess. You must have bought something while I wasn't there. Mr Horsforth was on duty so seldom that it was quite remarkable that you should have found him there at all. Now what, I wonder, was is that you bought?'

'I don't understand, my dear, this inquisitorial tone.'

'A hatpin!' I said. 'Maybe two? Half a dozen?'

'I don't think that, merely because one buys one of the *cheaper* articles on the stall—'

'Oh, I assure you that it isn't the price of the hatpins that I'm interested in,' I said. 'By no means. What concerns me is their strength. And their sharpness.'

Mrs Mipchin's mouth suddenly gaped most ungenteelly open.

'Why—?'

'Because it's my belief that one of Thyrza Primp's hatpins was used to stab Marcus.'

Elspeth Mipchin's teaspoon clattered on to her saucer with a sound that, in the silence, appeared deafening. She said in tones of great horror:

'Thyrza Primp's hatpins!'

And I said, rather in the manner of Banquo:

'Horrible, whoever's hatpin it was. But my mind keeps turning back to Thyrza Primp's, because they were strong, and old-fashioned, and available—and because it seems somehow appropriate. You do understand what I mean, don't you? When precisely did you buy yours?'

The strength seemed to have gone out of Elspeth Mipchin.

I think that normally she would have refused to answer, for she had the self-confidence of her own righteousness. But I had so disorientated her that her hand shook as she gave her tea an unnecessary stir, and she replied almost meekly:

'I don't know what time it was, but quite late. You had gone for lunch—I know, because Mr Horsforth was complaining about being left on his own.'

'What a hide,' I said calmly. 'So it must have been after two, then. You went up to the stall, and you bought—how many pins?'

'I bought half a dozen.' She rushed on: 'I bought six for Mary too.'

'Ah! Six for Mary Morse!'

'That's right. She had said earlier how useful they would be, but—'

'But she didn't want to come up and buy them while I was on the stall. Don't be embarrassed. I quite understand. So you got her some at the same time as you got your own. And when did you hand over your purchase to her?'

'Ah—er—not long afterwards. Mary was around in the tent—no, just outside. Mary had been listening to the choir . . . *such* a pretty performance!—and I handed them to her then and she gave me the 50p.'

'What time would this be?'

'Oh—ah—perhaps three, or a quarter past. Twenty past, even.'

'I see,' I said, feeling very much on top of things. Aggression was paying off. Elspeth Mipchin's hands were shaking still, I wasn't quite sure whether from guilt, or from a fear of Mary Morse. Either way, she was making no attempt to dispute my upper hand. I actually took from my handbag a little notebook and began to write things down.

'Right. Twelve hatpins accounted for—six in your possession, six in Mary Morse's. You'll have them still, I suppose? I think, you know, I'll have a look at them before I go. Now, since we have you equipped with a potential murder weapon, perhaps you'll tell me where you were, what you were doing, at the time when my husband was killed.'

'George—you shouldn't let her—'

'Really, Mrs Kitterege, this is a *little*—'

'If you prefer to talk to the Superintendent . . .' I said, making as if to go. This had an instant effect.

'Here!' said Elspeth Mipchin. 'We were here, weren't we, George?'

'That's right. Home from the fête. Er . . . what time *precisely* was it your poor husband . . .'

Again I had a disconcerting sense of amused eyes, coming at me from somewhere.

'Let's say between about a quarter to four and four.'

'We were having tea,' said Elspeth Mipchin flatly.

'Oh no, dear. We must be precise about this. Not on *Saturday*. Usually we would be having tea at that time. But we had lunched at The Green Knight—a very good cold meat and salad lunch they do there, and very cheap, or my good lady wouldn't normally like going to a public house. So since it was a day out, in a manner of speaking, we indulged ourselves a little. So when we got back from the fête, you remember, Elspeth, we said we'd just have a cup of tea and a scone at five o'clock.'

'Is that right?' I asked. There was an air of doom and retribution in the air, but Elspeth Mipchin could do nothing until I had gone. She nodded.

'So what did you both do?'

'Elspeth went upstairs to lie down on the bed. The day, you know, had been tiring and very hot, and she had to go back later for the clearing up. And I—wickedly, because as Elspeth says we do not usually approve of watching The Box in the daytime—I turned on the Second Test on the television. Such wonderfully entertaining players, the West Indians. A joy to watch.'

'So that in fact,' I said, 'you were not together—'

'*Not* together,' confirmed George Mipchin happily.

'In different parts of the house?'

'Quite.'

'And it would have been perfectly possible for one of you—?'

'One *or other* of us.'

'—to slip out and . . . get himself or herself along to Castle Walk.'

'Quite possible,' agreed George Mipchin. 'It's only a couple of minutes or so away.'

'Thank you,' I said. 'I enjoyed that tea very much indeed.'

CHAPTER 11

THYRZA AT THE VICARAGE

The vicarage that Walter and Thyrza Primp had moved into when they first arrived in Hexton to preach the gospel of middle-class morality was a large, be-creepered Victorian residence, suitable for a large family and a retinue of servants. It had long since been abandoned by the Church of England on the grounds that it was impossible to heat and hardly worth renovating. It was now owned by a writer— a man who constructed bestselling blockbusters with titles like *Corporation*, *Oil Rig* and *Palace*. He was occasionally to be seen with a pint of beer in The Green Knight, and he wrote letters to *The Times* over the address The Old Vicarage, which gave them double the chance of being published. He was currently rumoured to be engaged on a thousand-page epic called *Town Hall*, about steamy sex and corruption in British local government. We bought his books out of a sort of local patriotism, but he wasn't particularly Hexton.

Walter and Thyrza Primp, meanwhile, had removed themselves to the new vicarage which the Church had built for them (out of the rents derived from their brothel properties, the nastier minds in the town alleged). The new vicarage was a three-bedroomed affair, built in the local stone, but in a style best described as anonymous. 'It just suits us,' Walter Primp told everyone. And if Thyrza Primp regretted their two-peas-in-a-pod grandeur in the old vicarage, she had by then gained an unassailable position in the town, and her natural parsimony reconciled her to her reduced state. It was this vicarage, which over the years she had contrived to make as cluttered and claustrophobic as the old, that she was now leaving, to make way for Father Battersby.

When I called there, the next morning, I was not banking on a particularly cheery reception. Thyrza Primp, in fact, had never been notably hospitable, even during Walter's ministry: however lavish the spread provided—and it never was, particularly—she seemed to watch each item as it disappeared, as if she were operating some private system of rationing. In the event, however, my reception was even chillier than I had expected.

It began, of course, with Patch. I had left Jasper at home, foreseeing problems, but nevertheless Patch started away like a coloratura machine-gun the moment I put my finger on the bell. Patch had been brought up to repel vagrants and others who might call at the vicarage expecting charity, so he was only doing his duty, but he did it with rather too much of a will. Of course, a vet's wife must expect some of the odium to rub off on her where animals are concerned. As the barks soared into the stratosphere I was conscious of curtains being inched aside, and knew that when the door opened I would not present myself as any surprise.

In the event, the door merely inched open. Two black, piggy little eyes gleamed out from the murk inside. Patch threw himself at the crack, still doing his own particular version of the Mad Scene. The eyes inside glared, malicious and unyielding. The doormat on the step said 'Welcome'.

'Yes, Mrs Kitterege?'

'I've come to say goodbye, Thyrza,' I said, as if this were any old social call. 'I heard that you were leaving earlier than we all expected.'

'That's right,' came from the gloom, but no further social gesture was made.

'If you would just let Patch out—he knows me quite well, you know—it would be easier to talk.'

'Talk?' The implication was that there was nothing she would like less, but she opened it just a fraction, and Patch bowled out. He sniffed at my ankles, then rushed off to have a really good sniffle round the garden.

'I know you're busy—' I began.

'Very. *Very* busy. The removalists are coming to crate me up this afternoon.'

Images of cranes swinging Thyrza Primp, all crated up, into a container bound for Harrogate swam irresistibly into my mind. But I had to admit that I could hardly have called at a worse time. On the other hand, there was really no alternative, granted her advanced departure date.

'I wonder,' I said, 'if I might ask for just five minutes of your time—'

The door was allowed to swing open a little further, but only to allow Thyrza Primp to place her square, aggressive little body plumb in the opening. She was clad in a brown, crackly dress, and she looked like a paratrooper trained to repel all comers.

'No. I have no hesitation in saying NO. Sympathy in bereavement is one thing. I've always had that, I hope. And it's something I've needed myself very recently.' (I thought of mild little Walter Primp, whom a mild little heart attack had carried off to a mild little heaven, where I imagined him reading the *Daily Telegraph* and hoping that his relict was not to make the same journey in the too near future.) 'But I've no sympathy with sheer wrongheadedness. From all I've heard, you've gone clean out of your mind.'

'Perhaps I have,' I said. 'I've got the idea that my husband was murdered.'

'Yes, well, as I say, you have my sympathy. Though I may say that this is the first time *that's* happened to one of Walter's parishioners.'

'I'm also suffering from the delusion that I might help find out who killed him.'

'There you are, you see! That's what I heard. What nonsense! What dangerous nonsense! And I hear you also have got hold of the idea that it has to be one of us?'

'Yes. That is precisely what I do think. And please don't serve me up the soldiers again. The soldiers are a dead duck.'

'Then no doubt it was some unemployed vagrant.'

'Ah—the classical passing tramp. Really, I wonder how anyone ever dares pass a tramp. Well, you cling to that idea, Mrs Primp, and I'll cling to mine. What I'd like to ask—'

'No. Quite emphatically *no*. I hear you quite terrorized Elspeth Mipchin. An extraordinary procedure. She was *most* weak-minded to let it happen, and what her husband was thinking about, to just sit there while it was going on, I cannot imagine. Well, I assure you I am not going to let it happen to me. The idea! I've never heard of anything so undignified in my life!'

'Dignity is not something I'm thinking about much at the moment. But if you prefer to speak to the Superintendent . . .'

'Ha! Yes, I heard you were trying that one. Yes, I would prefer to talk to the Superintendent. I am not unaccustomed to dealing with the police. I had many occasions to do so during my late husband's ministry here.' (That was certainly true. Mrs Primp was anathema at the police station, due to her determination to view sin as synonymous with crime. Unwary vagrants, too, who called at the vicarage hoping for a hand-out were often disconcerted to find themselves up on a charge.) 'So don't try to terrify me with threats of the law!'

'Good. Well, I've no doubt he will want to talk to you. He was very interested this morning when I suggested that one of your hatpins might have been the murder weapon. A hatpin would correspond exactly to the nature of the injuries as set out in the autopsy, or so he said.'

'I should have thought that Mrs Culpepper was quite as likely a source of hatpins as myself, given her trade. But what if one of mine were used? They were not mine any more. I had handed them over—a charitable gesture, as I thought at the time, though precious few are the thanks I've received for it. I should have thought the police would be less interested in who had owned them in the past than in who had charge of them at the time of the murder. I should have thought, in fact, that the hatpins led them straight back not to me, but to you, Mrs Kitterege.'

She was clearly about to shut the door, having achieved this palpable hit, and I hurriedly said:

'Why are you leaving early, Mrs Primp?'

'Because the removalists changed the date they would collect my things. I have no more to say, so—'

'Do you ever feel sorry, Thyrza?' I asked, genuinely curious. 'Do you ever feel a twinge of conscience at the trouble you caused Marcus in the last weeks of his life? Do you regret all the silly rows and bitterness you stirred up in Hexton?'

As her face began to disappear in the gloom, something approaching a Cheshire Cat smile came over her face.

'I most certainly do not. If your husband had done his duty as a churchwarden, then none of this would have occurred. His trouble was lack of backbone. And that's the trouble with most of the people in this town. There's no one willing to stand up for what's right. That's all I've done. I've stood up for what's right.' I stood there silent, wondering what concluding cliché she would dish up. In the event, she favoured me with two ripe ones. 'My conscience is clear. I've nothing to reproach myself with.'

Patch, sensing the finality in her voice, did a racing-car swerve in through the front door, which was then shut, decisively, almost triumphantly, with that snapping 'Primp!' sound that I associated with Thyrza. I made my way down the front path, past the stocks and the hydrangeas, and out into the street.

The new vicarage had been built in a respectable but little-frequented corner of the town—quiet, unvisited by tourists. But houses it has—middle-class, net-curtained houses, and it was no doubt for this reason that, though there was no one else in the street, Timothy and Fiona, turning a corner, were already putting on a full performance even before they saw me: hands clasped winsomely behind their backs, long, lingering, doe-eyed looks into each other's eyes, giggling whispered confidences into each other's ears. I walked slowly towards them, anxious to witness the full range of their repertoire. I remembered that man in the P. G. Wodehouse story who keeps going up to people and whispering 'I know your secret.' I think I was miffed by my abject failure with Thyrza—anyway, something impelled me to try a variation on that idea. As I approached them, and as they apparently tore themselves from their absorbed and fascinated contemplation of each other to favour me with a double smile of unbearable innocence and sweetness, and before Timothy could address me with some words of sympathy which I'm sure he had been thinking up since he spotted me coming, I said:

'You really *don't* have to put on that performance just for my benefit, you know. I know all about you, you see.'

As I passed by, the smiles were still there, but they were like the smiles fixed on unfortunate faces by ill-starred operations in the early days of plastic surgery.

CHAPTER 12

SECRETS

It is, presumably, satisfying for the huntsman when a shot in the dark is rewarded by a yelp of pain. I certainly was inclined to preen myself when my shot in the dark resulted, just before lunch-time, in a phone call from Fiona Weston.

'Oh, I say, Mrs Kitterege, you did have us worried for a bit there, but after all, you're *not* going to say anything to anyone, are you, I mean, parents or anyone, because after all it's not relevant to anything. I mean, not to your husband's death, I mean—gosh—how could it be? and we know you're looking into it, and we think it's jolly clever of you, and brave, but our little private goings-on have *nothing* to do with anything like that, and we do hope you'll keep them under your hat, because—Gosh, here comes the Pops, I must fly, but you *won't*, will you—?'

Fiona, it seemed, had been caught by her charade in a 'twenties groove. What was rather annoying was that her call had given me no shred of a clue as to what I was supposed to know. Beyond the fact that at that age the secret was likely to revolve around sex, I had no inkling.

I said as much to Franchita Culpepper when I called on her that same day for afternoon tea. She was the only one who attempted to say—sincerely, I felt sure—how sorry she was about Marcus, and how much the town was going to miss him. The effect of her words was rather blunted by Oscar, who jumped up at me, butted me with his head and his rump, and licked all available areas of bare skin to express his mountainous delight at my visit. It's no joke being jumped up at by a nearly full-grown Rottweiler, but he nicely covered the embarrassment we all feel, in Hexton, at the expression of any sort of emotion.

'Come to ask questions?' roared Franchita, retreating into her more normal mode of conversation as we went into the sitting-room. It was a room I had always liked. The house had been owned for decades by an old lady who expected to die at any moment, but never did, and who consequently did as little as possible in the way of redecoration or renewal of furniture. Franchita, presumably with Howard's help, had made it a little museum of Art Deco, with all sorts of knick-knacks and oddities of the period scattered around (some worth many times, now, what they had paid for them, though I should imagine that was usually true of anything Franchita bought). In this Coward-like setting Franchita, I suspect, saw herself as an Amanda, though in fact she was more like Madame Arcati.

'To ask questions, yes,' I said. 'How things get around.'

'Is there any small town where they don't? Howard's out, by the way.'

I was glad. It seemed to give me a freer hand with Franchita. But I was so unused to his having any existence or activity separate from Franchita's that there was probably surprise in my voice when I asked:

'What's he doing?'

'Teaching Russian at the army camp.'

'I didn't know Howard knew Russian.'

'Of course he does. That's what he taught at Grimsby University, before they cut out Russian. Can you imagine a government being so stupid as to step up the Cold War and cut down on Russian teaching at the same time? That's what this one did. I wouldn't vote for the silly woman except that there *is* nobody else to vote for. Howard is Russian language—nouns and declensions and irregular verbs and all that. Doesn't need any imagination, which is a damn good thing, because he hasn't got any. Howard's just what the army needs. I used to teach English once, but it was *literature.* Tea? Cake? I'll see what's in the tin.'

While she was away foraging in the kitchen, I patted Oscar and tried to fit Howard Culpepper's teaching of Russian into a pattern that could have led to the killing of Marcus. I failed dismally. I could imagine Franchita, in her youth, as a seductive and steely-willed spy, seducing secrets out of National Servicemen, but *that* didn't seem to lead me any closer to Marcus's death either.

'Damned glad Howard's got this job,' said Franchita, coming back with trays. 'Minding him all day becomes a bit of a chore after a time. He's out there three afternoons a week, which gets him out of my hair, quite apart from bringing in a welcome little bit of money.'

'I never thought of you as in need of money.'

'We're not. We'd just like *more*.' She flashed her molars at me. 'Howard was paid off handsomely, though that doesn't remove the sting. I've got a little bit of my own. Still, hat shops don't exactly bring in a fortune. I charge the earth—as you've no doubt noticed—and the new people always come and buy from me when they find out that hats are still *de rigueur* here. But they don't buy new ones every season, as people once did, and the young ones buy their jokey hats at jumble sales. No—I'd have done better to have gone in for video games, or some such darned thing. Wouldn't I have kept those little blighters in order!'

Her smile was at its most fearsome. I wondered why I liked her, and thought it must be her honesty and self-knowledge.

'I went to see Thyrza today,' I said.

'How brave of you. I'm saying my farewells to her by card: I don't want to be upbraided as a renegade. But of course you had an added motive for going.'

'I did.'

'Hatpins?'

'Hatpins among other things.'

'Hatpins,' said Franchita, thoughtfully stirring her tea, 'stick rather closely home.'

'That was a point that dear Thyrza made quite forcefully. As a source for hatpins your shop is quite as likely as the little collection of her old ones on my stall.'

'Quite. And the more one thinks about it, your idea about hatpins, though quite brilliant as an *aperçu*, doesn't exactly narrow the field, does it? Thyrza Primp invariably wears some horrific creation secured to her hair by a pin. Mary Morse hardly less often. The ladies of Hexton—all those of a certain age, anyway—*have* hats of that sort, every one of them, even if they only wear them from time to time. And the men of Hexton are all husbands, are they not? Very *much* so, one feels. So they'd have access to hatpins.'

'Not Mr Horsforth.'

'But Mr Horsforth looked after your stall from time to time. So there you are.'

'But if this thing was an impulse murder—and surely one would never *choose* a hatpin as a weapon, not with premeditation—then it surely points to a woman. A man wouldn't have one *on* him.'

'Do men have similar things? Cigar pins, or something like that? And of course one of our husbands might have been taking one home for his wife, or carrying her purchases. No, I can't see that it narrows it down. I'm taking the cast list of suspects, you see, at your own valuation, and assuming it wasn't some passing nut, like the Pink Panter.'

The Pink Panter was our name for one of the local compulsive joggers, jogging away the boredom and miseries of unemployment. He was in his fifties, and habitually very pink indeed.

'The Pink Panter certainly wouldn't be likely to have a hatpin on him,' I conceded. 'He always looks regrettably without support of any kind. Yes, I'm resisting all idea of passing tramps, passing nuts and passing tourists with sudden homicidal urges.'

'Well, then, if you're really looking for the key in these shenanigans of the last few weeks—of my part in which I'm most sincerely ashamed—then presumably you've got to look to the ones who had most call to feel defeated and resentful.'

'Obviously. The opposition.'

'Thyrza and Mary, the Mipchins—'

'And you, Franchita. Precisely. Why did you say just now that you were ashamed?'

'Well, it's hardly something one is likely to feel proud of.'

'You don't give a damn about the Church. You only come once in a blue moon. Why did you get involved?'

'Boredom, I suppose. When I married Howard—he's my third, you know, apart from "other compaignye in youthe,"—I thought: "All right, he's dull, and he'll knuckle under so easily there won't be any pleasure in the struggle, but at least there'll be the university to give a bit of spice to life." And of course, it *did*: university people are so openly and unashamedly frightful, and there is all the intrigue and conspiracy and backbiting, so that life always keeps chugging along very amusingly. And then suddenly—poof —and it was over. And we were just *fairly* well off, in a rather dull little town, with a shop that not many people come into. So the fight over Father Battersby seemed to revive all that university in-fighting which I'd so enjoyed, and gave a bit of spice to life. But I *am* ashamed, and I'll make it up to the poor man: I shall be so *fearsomely* hospitable and protective that he'll run a mile when he sees me coming down the street.'

'As people do from me at the moment. "Unclean! Unclean! Suffering from grief!" It's a very uncomfortable feeling.'

'Hexton isn't too easy with the life of the emotions.'

'No, indeed. Hence its need to resort to all sorts of shifts. By the way, Timothy and Fiona passed me today, and I was so infuriated by their act—perhaps it was the jealousy of the newly widowed, do you think?—that I said: "Don't put on that act just for me. I know all about you." The effect has been extraordinary.'

'Really?'

'Fiona ringing up and making all sorts of incoherent noises about I won't tell Daddy, will I, and so on.'

'Frankly, I'd have thought Fiona could twist Colonel Weston round her little finger with no problem at all. Mummy might be more of a problem—mummies always are. Timothy's another matter, of course. Once one knows the whole gooey performance is an act, one is inclined to look more favourably on that pair, and want them to get away with it a little bit longer, don't you think? I am not inclined greatly to like Headmaster Horsforth. Under that bleak exterior there lurks a bleak interior. A born tyrant in the home, I shouldn't wonder.'

'Oh, no question, I'd say. I can see the lad must have his problems, which might excuse his acting a role, if not overacting it so disgustingly. But I must say I found the whole episode generally interesting: it suggested that the secrets of Hexton respectables might be a fascinating further field for investigation.'

This was the sort of idea that was likely to appeal to Franchita.

'Enticing possibilities seem to open up,' she said. 'Like Thyrza Primp's long-concealed lover in Harrogate.'

'Quite,' I said. 'Or yours in Barnard's Castle.'

I'm never quite sure whether Oscar at this point stirred from his snoozing place beside the table, or whether an involuntary movement from Franchita overturned it: both Oscar and Franchita were potentially lethal to occasional tables. At any rate, over it went—cups, plates, the lot, and though a thick, handwoven rug ensured that nothing much was broken, still an undoubted diversion was caused.

'Damn. Oscar, you're a menace. Christ, look at that cream cake all over the rug. Lick it up, boy. You don't really want cream cake, do you, Helen? Here, have a chocolate instead. Rather amusing, the box, eh?'

She handed me a 'thirties box of Princess Elizabeth and Princess Margaret Rose chocolates, with sweet, coy pictures of the little princesses themselves on the top.

'The chocolates are new, of course.'

'How amusing,' I said. 'The Palace would never allow that today, more's the pity. We could have a Princess Anne chocolate box—all hard centres. Come on, Franchita, I know you're stalling for time. Tell me about Barnard's Castle.'

Franchita's habitual bellicosity was distinctly softened by now, but she was not one to be driven into a corner without protest.

'What the hell makes you think there's anything to tell? All sorts of people prefer to have their professional men from outside the town. I bet there are heaps of people in Hexton who didn't use Marcus as their vet.'

'I really don't know. Lots of animals hardly ever need a vet at all.'

'If you go outside the town it saves awkwardnesses: you change your dentist because you think he's ham-fisted, then you're always meeting him at sherry parties and things. Damned unpleasant. No—it makes sense to go outside.'

'Come off it, Franchita. You might go to Barnard's Castle for your dental treatment without arousing suspicion, but there's no earthly reason for your staying overnight, which you do every time. It's no distance at all from here. Now—don't go all coy. Spill the beans.'

Franchita gave me one of her most tradesman-quelling glances, but her heart wasn't in it, and, seeing it had no effect on me, she struggled with her facial muscles and gave me a terrifying grin instead.

'Oh, what the hell. Yes, well, we are sort of friends, the dentist and me. He was one of the "other compaignye in youthe" I mentioned. Always kept contact—damned good fun, to tell you the truth, which Howard *isn't*, always.'

'And you have regular meetings?'

'Well, yes. Combining it with a check-up—which obviously you find very funny, but it just happens to be convenient. Anyway, sometimes something happens, sometimes it doesn't, because he has a wife, and he's getting on a bit, but either way it's a bit of a diversion. Relief from the monotony.'

'And Howard knows?'

'Haven't the faintest idea. If so, he's gentleman enough not to say. May have noticed that I say I go for a check-up every six months, whereas really it's more like four. May have—and then again, may not have: not all *that* bright, Howard.'

'Not all that dim either, though. You Hexton wives always assume that because you've got the upper hand, you've got a devoted, unquestioning lifelong slave. It ain't, as Sportin' Life says, necessarily so.'

'Maybe not. Really, I'd rather like to have Howard rebel. It'd be sort of like the uprising in the Warsaw ghetto—heroic and hopeless. But I can't see it happening.'

'Or *he* could have an affair.'

'I'd like to see him try!'

'Perhaps, though, he is already. In fact, perhaps everyone in Hexton has their little secrets, of this kind or some other. That's what I find so interesting about my lucky hit with Timothy and Fiona.'

'I've no doubt *many* of them have secrets—*everyone* might be going a bit far. I mean, Thyrza Primp makes a virtue of all her awfulnesses, so she has no reason to make secrets of them. She implies that anyone without those awfulnesses is somehow lowering the standard.'

'Would you say Mary Morse was in that category?'

'Mary? She's not quite the same kind of case, is she? In fact, she's interesting. One would hardly suggest that Mary could have a lover. On the other hand, she might have some kind of social secret—something she doesn't want known. Because to Mary position in the town is everything: what would she be without it but a boring and middle-aged woman without enough to do with her time? So there's likely to be something she would like to keep quiet, because there is in most families that value their position. The brothers? Could it be the brothers, now?'

'I know nothing about them.'

'No, quite. Nobody does. And *sons* are normally rather prized in Hexton—pathetic though most of the menfolk here are. Yet it's many years since either the one or the other has been so much as mentioned by Mary, so far as I can make out. Yes—I'd plump for the brothers.'

'It's a thought. In fact, family is a more likely source of guilty secrets in Hexton, where everyone is so old, than sex. You get past one, but never the other. But most of us have moved here, and that makes it more difficult: if the Primps have a secret in their family, it's no doubt well behind them in their past. Similarly with Mr Horsforth. Though I must say I would like to find out some really juicy secret about him.'

'Oh, certainly—but that applies to Thyrza and the Mipchins too, though I really can't believe in one in either case.'

'Speculation,' I said, stirring in my chair, 'doesn't seem likely to get us much further.'

'Oh, don't go, Helen. Have another chocolate.'

Franchita pressed on me a fat and milky specimen from the Little Princesses box, but I refused.

'Just one more thing: did you notice when Thyrza Primp left the fête on Saturday?'

'Oh—I *should* know. She came up and gave me tight-lipped thanks for organizing it, as if she were still vicar's wife. I don't know whose condescension was worse—hers, or Mary's or Lady Godetia's. Let me see, it was not that late in the afternoon. Mary, I know, was still there, because she was fawning over Lady Godetia in the background. I'd say it must have been about two o'clock.'

'Right. My impression was that she wasn't around as the afternoon wore on. Whereas you, of course, Franchita, were there all the time.'

She bared her teeth at me, and put her big, strong hands on her hips.

'Of course. *You* know that. I was here, there and everywhere all day, making my presence felt. If I'd disappeared for twenty minutes or half an hour, people really would have noticed!'

Or would they, I wondered, merely have breathed a sigh of relief, and assumed that someone else in some other part of the tent was getting it in the neck? It really wouldn't do to rule out Franchita on those grounds alone.

CHAPTER 13

DELUSIONS OF GRANDEUR

To open the high gate in the walled garden of Mary Morse's house, to go up the front path towards the whitewashed porch, was to feel that I had come full circle. There, once again, was Roote, bedding out stocks with a geometrical precision that had doubtless been enjoined upon him; there was the ugly, stonedashed house, put up for himself in the 'twenties by a builder with pretensions and a large family; there were the brass mud-scrapers on the doorstep. Inside, no doubt, the souvenirs of the Holy Land were kept immaculately dust-free, and the favourite novel by Angela Thirkell was waiting to be returned to the library after a third or fourth re-reading. I remembered what an appalling old bitch Thirkell seems to have been, and thought what an appropriate read for Miss Mary Morse: the icy heart beneath the social veneer.

À propos of social veneers, I remembered that my last

words to Mary Morse had been 'God damn and blast you all to Hell,' or some such formulation. Some bridging seemed to be necessary before a social call could get off on a fruitfully companionable footing—and after my experience with Thyrza I decided that that was about the only way I could play it this time. Thus, when I had saluted Roote, who gave me a suitably gnarled greeting, as if he were acting in a TV adaptation of a Victorian novel, I composed my face into a hypocritical mask, and when the door opened to my ring, I said:

'Mary—I think I owe you an apology. I wasn't myself when you rang the other day.'

God forgive me for a liar. I even smiled wanly. Mary Morse was clearly taken aback. She was obviously expecting my visit, but equally obviously she had been anticipating a more aggressive approach. She too smiled, with a fusty sweetness.

'Of course, Helen dear. I *quite* understand. Won't you come in? So lucky you called at tea-time.'

I went in—into the varnishy hall, smelling of old over-coats and furniture polish. The book on the hallstand turned out to be an R. F. Delderfield. The pile on the hall carpet was so immaculately fluffed up, so completely devoid of grime or grit, that I felt I ought to be offered overshoes, as in a Moslem holy place. The feeling of hushed holiness was augmented by a photograph of old Mrs Morse, presiding over a table of vegetable marrows at some long-ago harvest festival, stood in a place of honour on the stand: she had an expression of aggressive triumph on her face, and the marrows looked like nothing so much as cannons trained on an invisible enemy. It was not the most welcoming photograph Mary could have chosen for her hall.

We went into the sitting-room, lighter than when I had seen it last. Mary was wearing the same drab grey dress as she had had on then: as I suspected, she had anticipated my coming, and this was her wear for funerary parties. She left me for a moment to put on a kettle. How much more appropriate, I thought, if Mary had had a little maid to bully and to train up in the ways of gentility. Who knows —with so much teenage unemployment, Mary might yet manage it. The times were ripe for a return to semi-serfdom.

When Mary returned from the kitchen, with a plate of cakes and one of sandwiches that must have been prepared in advance 'in case', she had got her little speech nicely prepared:

'I don't want to say too much, Helen, or to open up wounds that are healing, but *how* we are all going to miss Marcus. Sophronia Tibbles *instinctively* knows, I'm sure of it. I can't *think* who I'm to take her to now.'

Sophronia Tibbles gazed balefully at her mistress from a chair in the corner, as if she resented having human feelings attributed to her by so foolish a human as her mistress.

'Simon Fox is an excellent vet,' I said.

'But the sympathy, my dear, the quiet sympathy, the warmth of understanding that Marcus had for animals . . .'

'He did have a very good basket-side manner,' I said briskly. But I pulled myself back. I intended this interview to retain at least a patina of the Hexton conventionalities, so I certainly shouldn't show my sharper side too early. I added: 'You're quite right. The animals will miss him.'

So it was Marcus the vet we were missing, was it, I thought, as Mary went back to the kitchen. Not a word about Marcus the churchwarden. Was she going to keep the conventionalities on pussies and doggies for the entire visit? Not if I could help it.

'It's a gift,' said Mary determinedly, coming back with a tray of cups and jugs. 'And Marcus just had it.'

'Quite,' I said. 'And he was very good with humans too, you know, though he did feel he had failed with them, over the last few weeks of his life.'

'Don't you think, my dear,' said Mary, who was presiding over the pouring, and who had assumed an expression of ineffable complacency, 'that that is a subject that we would do best to avoid? When is the funeral to take place?'

I bit into a sandwich. Cress again. Mary must have registered how much I disliked it.

'I really don't know. When the police release the body.'

'And will his family come? Isn't his father a clergyman? So very appropriate, I always thought.'

'A dead clergyman, I'm afraid. But his mother is still alive, and he had brothers and sisters. Yes, I'm sure they'll all come.' I added, since this gave me an opening: 'Family can be helpful on such occasions—if they're the right sort of family. It must have been trying, for you, being on your own.'

'But of course I couldn't have expected Philip to come— not from Australia,' Mary replied hurriedly.

'I suppose you couldn't. And John—?'

'Couldn't come. Have a sandwich, dear. So interesting that Marcus in a way grew up in the Church—'

In her haste to escape from the topic of her brothers, Mary had plunged into the very subject she had suggested we avoid.

'Quite,' I said. 'Tinged with the ecclesiastic from birth. One of his brothers, in fact, went into a monastery—'

'Ah!' said Mary significantly. 'He *went over*, did he?'

'Oh, only on a short visit. He found he had no vocation. Now he teaches the *Marxism Today* course for the Open University. He really had very little in common with Marcus. Marcus, you know, was never one for extremes.'

'No, quite. An ability to smooth over differences is so valuable—though of course it's dangerous if it leads to *compromises*.'

'That, surely, is what it normally has to lead to.'

'But some of us—I don't think your Marcus always understood this, or sympathized—some of us are people of con*viction*. We know that in some areas there *can* be no compromise—that compromise is an abdication of responsibility.' (Oh God—she's getting a Thatcher complex, I thought.) 'Our little differences—and I hope they were never more than that, and that they didn't become *personal* in any way—came about precisely for that reason. I did not believe that we could allow the Bishop to foist on us a man who is virtually a priest—positively a Catholic priest! It was a matter of faith, and the practice of that faith, so naturally there could be no compromise.'

'Fortunately,' I said, with the intention of provoking, 'that little matter seems to have sorted itself out now. Most people seem to have accepted Father Battersby quite happily.'

'Oh no, dear.' Again that aggravating little smile of complacent knowing-better. 'I don't think you'll find that is so. Of course, on Sunday people were upset and confused —quite understandably so. But I've been doing my best, stiffening resolves—'

'I'm sure you have—'

'—and you'll find that next week we shall see a quite different picture emerge. I know you can't have a great deal of sympathy with me, Helen dear, over this, having been brought up in a quite different spiritual tradition, or perhaps really none at all, isn't that right, dear? But it's something I know in my bones I have to do. As one of the leaders of this little community.'

Self-proposed and self-elected, I thought.

'I'm afraid,' I said, 'that I've always had a tendency to distrust leaders.'

'I know you have, Helen dear. You've always made that quite clear, but you nevertheless are wrong. People in the mass are so easily confused, so readily get hold of the wrong end of the stick, so easily miss the *ethical* point. You'll find, if you look around, that each little community throws up a few natural leaders.'

'And you think Hexton has thrown up you?'

'Perhaps in some degree you might say that I inherited

the position,' she said, undented in her self-approval, and pressing another cress sandwich on me as a sign that she forgave my tone. 'Though I hope it may be said too that I managed to make my own little contribution to the community's welfare, even while poor Mother was alive. Now, with Thyrza about to depart, it is clear that a very *special* kind of responsibility is going to fall on my shoulders. People will be looking up to me more and more for guidance.' (Oh God—a Pope complex, I thought.) 'I accept the challenge. I do not intend to disappoint them.'

'Mary,' I asked, 'what were you doing in the later stages of Saturday afternoon?'

'Ah—' she said, with another forbearing smile. 'I thought you were going to ask that. I know that Thyrza took a strong line with you over the matter. But I feel we ought to make allowances. It's natural you should take an interest.'

'Good of you,' I murmured.

'Well, on Saturday, as you know, I arrived at the fête around midday, I think, and of course I went around in the tent a great deal—up and down the aisles, having a word here, a word there. People who've put in voluntary effort need a pat on the back, don't you feel? And I went around, showing my appreciation.' (A Lady Godetia complex, I thought.) 'And of course I bought a little something here, bestowed a word of praise there, trying to do my little bit. That took me up to—let me see—about three or so.'

'You talked,' I said (avoiding the phrase 'had a session' only by inches), 'with Lady Godetia.'

'Quite. Dear Godetia. Community business, you know. *Such* an interest she takes, though I do sometimes feel in her case that the spiritual dimension is lacking. Where was I? Oh yes, three o'clock. Well, about then, or possibly a shade later, I went outside, watching the various games, talking a little to members of the choir—*weren't* they good this year? —and, let me see . . .'

'You talked to Marcus?'

'Yes! Precisely. I talked to Marcus. Dreadful to think that I was one of the last to see him alive.'

'Yes, dreadful. Where was this, and what did you both say?'

'Oh dear—I have to be precise about this, though in fact the police have asked me about it as well. Now, I'd been down to the river, to talk to one of the mothers—she was letting her little girl bathe *naked* in the river, and though it was only a tot, we all know there are people, terrible people, who can so easily be given *ideas* . . . And of course she saw my point. After that, I was strolling back towards the games, when I saw Marcus walking *away* from the fête, and the games, quite fast . . .'

'Walking *after* someone, do you mean?'

'I really couldn't say, dear. There were people all around, coming and going. I just assumed he was wanting to get back home, to have a little break from his duties.'

'So there wasn't anyone in particular there that he could have been walking after?'

Mary wrinkled her forehead, as if genuinely in thought. Perhaps she would have liked to remember someone.

'No . . . No, I can't say I noticed anyone in particular. Anyway, what I wanted to emphasize was that Marcus seemed in a hurry, and that was why we didn't exchange many words . . . Because I *hope* we weren't on such terms that we couldn't have a pleasant conversation, should the occasion arise.'

'But as it was   ?'

'As it was, Marcus smiled, and I smiled, and I think he said what a pleasant day it was, and . . . wasn't the fête going well, and I said yes, and . . . that was it. Positively it.'

'And then Marcus hurried on?'

'Yes. Or at least I suppose so.'

'And you?'

'I went back towards the games . . . congratulated some

of the contestants—rough lads, some of them, but respectful in their dumb kind of way . . . then I had a word with Mr Horsforth . . . well, quite a conversation, it was, really. About the declining standards of dress at the Grammar School. I know times are said to be hard, but I *cannot* understand how parents can send their children to school in jeans. Jeans! Mr Horsforth agreed with me, of course . . . And then I came home.'

'When would that be?'

'Well, really, dear, I didn't time myself. But I think I was home by about a quarter past four. I know I had afternoon tea as soon as I got in.'

'I see,' I said.

My mind was chewing over this information. If Marcus had gone straight up Castle Wynd and along Castle Walk, then he was probably killed while Mary was having her conversation (assuming she was speaking the truth) with Mr Horsforth. If, on the other hand, he had done something else—what?—first, then he could have met up with Mary again along Castle Walk. Yet Castle Walk was on the way home neither for Mary nor for Marcus.

'And you stayed at home then?'

'Yes. Oh, but of course later, when I heard—'

'Who told you?'

'Franchita, I think. Yes it was. Poor Franchita: how terrible for *her* fête to end in that way. She was there, too, you know. She *saw*—'

'I was there. I saw.'

'I *know*, dear. That's why we . . . make allowances. So after I heard, I thought a little, and of course it occurred to me that I just might have been one of the last to see Marcus alive. Now, whatever you may say about me, Helen dear, I am not one to shirk my duty, so I went to the police—'

'You *went* there—?'

'Well, dear, the telephone is never quite satisfactory for these things, is it? Yes, I put my coat on, and went to the police station there and then, and told them my little all, though I couldn't see how it could be really important. Anyway, they were most polite and grateful—the Superintendent it was I talked to, of course . . . and I gave them some words of encouragement and support, and told them how Hexton *as a whole* was behind them in their search for this killer.'

Back to Mrs Thatcher, I thought, visiting the police after a bomb outrage. Were Mary Morse's delusions funny, or frightening?

'You also,' I said brutally, 'mentioned Lady Godetia.'

'Lady Godetia?' she echoed, looking at me wide-eyed, with an expression of innocent astonishment on her face. 'Oh no. I don't think so. What reason could there have been to mention her? No, Helen dear, I think you must have been misinformed there. So *many* people out to cause trouble, aren't there? And then of course I came home and went to bed. Such a tiring day, you know.'

'Quite. I found it tiring myself. And the next day you and Thyrza went on your bus to wherever-it-was, for your church service?'

'We did, dear, and I am *not* going to get annoyed by your tone of voice, and I assure you that we were not put out in any way that more did not come with us.' The smile of complacent pity for the weakness of lesser men was fixed rather frighteningly on her face. 'Great oaks from little acorns, you know. We blazed a trail. I have had many assurances from people who will be following that trail next week. That is what leadership is about, you know. I'm always conscious, in everything I do, that people are looking to me to set a certain standard, and are looking to me for guidance, *moral* guidance. It's a terrible burden and responsibility, but I accept it gladly. In every community there has to be someone to set the standard, someone on whom the rest can model themselves.'

Queen Mary, I thought! Old Queen Mary! As she

sat there, ramrod-straight, with that smile of regal self-absorption on her face, I really felt rather frightened. I looked round the room, preparatory to getting up. I'd been aware since I came in that something had been changed in the arrangement since I'd sat here last. Virtually nothing else had—the room was practically a museum to the tastes and habits of Mary's mother, a Morse-oleum—but one thing had. That was it! On the sideboard there was now only one photograph of a Morse boy, not the two that had been there before. As I got up to go, I casually went over and picked it up.

'Your brother Philip,' I said.

'That's right,' said Mary edgily.

The picture showed a bronzed and grinning man, in an open-necked shirt, standing outside a very extensive, positively palatial house. I had been to Australia as a teenager, to visit relatives. It didn't fool me.

'Vaucluse House,' I said.

'I beg your pardon?'

'Vaucluse House. It's the nearest thing they have in New South Wales to a stately home. Historic monument, you know.'

'Oh,' said Mary. She sounded disappointed. I really think she had convinced herself that it was her brother Philip's home.

All the time I had been looking around the room for the missing photograph. Finally I spotted it, in a dark corner over by the piano. Mary had been willing to move it into obscurity, but not so far to change the Mother-given order of things as to remove it entirely. I could feel Mary's irritation coming over me in waves as I strolled over and picked it up. It was a graduation photograph, the product of a studio, perhaps in the mid-'sixties. John Morse stood on a studio step in cap and gown. Clearly he was not enjoying the experience, was going through with it only because he had been commanded to. He gazed ahead, aggressive, somehow cunning, and to my mind saying something like: 'I'm going to get even with you for this.'

'What university?' I asked.

'Grimsby,' snapped Mary.

'Really? Howard Culpepper's university. What did he graduate in?'

'Sociology.'

She said it as if it were a dirty word. At last something that Mary and I might agree on. I put the picture down.

'Well, thank you *so* much, Mary, for the tea, and for being so helpful generally . . .'

As we made our goodbyes, some semblance of a normal social relationship in Hexton terms was re-established, and I think that as she closed the door Mary was probably congratulating herself that she had handled things *so* much better than poor dear Thyrza. But then Mary, the new Mary, seemed to congratulate herself on just about everything. She had elevated herself into a nonpareil. Proceedings for sainthood would be initiated shortly.

The first thing I said to myself as I walked slowly and thoughtfully home was: Mary is mad. Of course I meant this in the slack, general way people do use the word, but on reflection I wasn't at all sure that it mightn't develop into a literal, clinical madness. There was the fact that Mary had apparently re-ordered the events of the fête day in her mind in such a way that it had become a triumph for her: she had gone round graciously congratulating and graciously thanking, and the unlettered peasants had shown inarticulate gratitude and devotion. Murder had apparently not been able to dim the truly royal glow that the event now cast in her mind's eye. Such re-writing of history could spring only from the mind of a politician, a Marxist historian, or from a mind in the grip of a personal delusion.

Then there were the other delusions of her power and influence—the moral presidency of the town that she had mentally elected herself to. This was a figure infinitely grander than the moral busybody that Mary had always genuinely been. This new figure set the tone, led the way, laid down the moral law; she was a force for stability and order. This in the face of her total rejection by Hexton both on the day of the fête, and the day after. One could truly say: That way madness lies—but had madness perhaps come already?

Then there was the matter of the brother. *Could* that in any way be relevant? The likelihood was that it was one of the perfectly normal family secrets that people habitually prefer not to be talked about, and Mary would like less than most to have discussed: jail, bankruptcy . . . lunacy.

But something worth killing Marcus for, if Marcus had found out? And *how* had Marcus found something like that out? And if he had done, wouldn't he have told me?

Well, no: quite likely he would not have told me. Marcus didn't talk readily about other people's affairs (it was his greatest fault), and he didn't like the relish with which I uncovered the seamy underbelly of Hexton life. But then, granted Marcus's tact and charity, how did Mary know that he knew? Because one thing was certain: he would never have mentioned it to her.

And there was something else. Something Mary had said, that had clicked in my mind. Something that reminded me of something someone had said on some other social occasion. Mary herself? Or someone else? What the hell was it? I hadn't taken a notebook to Mary's, thinking to establish a rather pleasanter social atmosphere than I had at the Mipchins', and on the whole I had been successful. Now I regretted it, though. Except that the thing had been such a little thing that I probably would not have noted it down anyway. Such a very little thing . . .

CHAPTER 14

AT LI CHEN'S

There was this to be said for Hexton's custom of making calls on the bereaved after a death, over mine of the bereaved making the calls herself: with Hexton's system, the bereaved could make her own choice of funeral baked meats. I felt I would get very tired of lemon fingers and unidentifiable sandwiches without benefit of crust before very long. Thin bread and butter would be vastly preferable, and muffins positively comforting.

On the Thursday, though, a variation on this round, this series of dismal tributes to the attenuated custom of the English tea-time, occurred to me. On Thursdays Lady Godetia's cook at Walworth, her manor house seven miles from town, had the day off, and Lady Godetia drove erratically into Hexton, in a manner that seemed to presuppose an armed escort to clear the motorway before and behind, and ate lunch at Li Chen's. I had no great hopes of anything of any value coming from a chat with Lady Godetia: her name's coming into the case at all was a matter of mischief-making on Mary's part, springing from her need to divert attention from her own doings in the weeks before Marcus's death. Lady Godetia had no interest in church matters: her attendance at Edward the Confessor's was occasional and social, and none of the churches near Walworth saw her any more often. Added to that, she had no doubt spent the entire afternoon of Saturday being gracious in the tent. Nevertheless, Mary had made Godetia part of the case, and to Li Chen's I would go.

Actually, Hexton's Chinese restaurant rejoices in the name of The Jasmine Pavilion, but we always called it Li

Chen's, with an intonation that might either be familiar or colonial-lordly. As soon as I got in the door, I saw I had rather miscalculated my time: Lady Godetia was already seated at a table under the windows, surrounded by a series of dishes on plate-warmers, all of them three-parts consumed. Lady Godetia, under the powder-blue coats and feathery hats, was a heavy nosher. When he saw me at the door, Li Chen bustled forward and offered consolation in his way by being, momentarily, his natural self.

'I was real sorry to hear about Mr Kitterege, Mrs K. He was a lovely person, no kidding. Try the king prawn today, eh? They're beaut.'

As I made appropriate response, I edged towards the window, and Mr Li reverted happily to his restaurant self: 'You like table near window? You like nice glass led wine?'

Li Chen was a terrible fraud, who was not above saying 'flied lice' if the fancy took him.

As we approached Lady Godetia's, it became clear that my tactic was going to pay off, though it did so in a way rather different from my intention. Looking up to wipe sweet and sour sauce from her chin, she witnessed my approach and waved.

'Oh—Mrs—er—How nice to see you! Do come and join me while I finish my bits and pieces. You're looking a little peaky. You must have overdone things at the fête. *So* tiring, aren't they? Though this year's was *such* a success, thanks to all you busy people.'

It was quite clear that she had only the vaguest idea who I was. Her card-index, consulted no doubt on the night before the fête, must have been put out of her mind immediately afterwards. If I had ever had any notion that there might be substance in Mary's preposterous suggestion, then this would have dispelled it. If Lady Godetia had had anything going with Marcus, then she would have made sure she knew who Marcus's wife was. Not that I had ever had the faintest twinge of doubt on that score. If Marcus had had, or was having, an affair—and maybe he had . . . maybe he was—then I paid him the compliment of absolute confidence that it would not have been with Lady Godetia.

There seemed little point in sitting down with her now, but I did so, and got what pleasure I could from pricking a little pin into her social manner.

'In point of fact I didn't enjoy the fête all that much,' I said.

'Oh. That murder. No, most unfortunate, poor man . . . Oh! . . . Oh dear! Oh, darling—you're *not* . . . Oh, but I didn't imagine you could be out so soon . . . How *can* I apologize enough? Really, *what* must you think of my clumsiness?'

Colour had come into her cheeks, already heated with her eating. She seemed almost genuinely upset, as very social people can be over a *faux pas*. I waved her back to her lunch as I ordered king prawns and a chow mein and a glass of wine from Mr Li. After a moment's hesitation, and a desperate search for something to say to retrieve the situation, Lady Godetia bent down to gobble at a plate of pork and ginger, apparently intent on being gone as soon as possible.

'My dear,' she said, still pink with embarrassment as Li Chen departed with my order. 'I didn't, I really *didn't*, mean to imply that the fête was a success as a whole. I really *hadn't* forgotten your poor husband, and that dreadful scene —*stamped* on my memory, I do assure you. Because he really was a *great* favourite of mine, you know . . . It's just that I thought you were one of the ordinary helpers, and I ought to say something . . . cheery.'

'That's all right,' I said, extra cool as usual in the face of her mannered gush.

'We cancelled my speech at the end, you know,' Godetia said, as if that were the ultimate proof of their sincerity.

'Never mind,' I said. 'You can probably make it next year.'

Lady Godetia gave renewed signs of wanting very much to get away. Much more of me and she might even leave something uneaten.

'You actually saw the body float by, did you?' I said, rather as if I were a reporter questioning one of the knights or dames of Camelot about the end of the Lady of Shalott's voyage.

'Well, yes, actually. Everyone seemed to go out there, so I, eventually, followed. So appalling, and so strange. I *dreamt* about it that night.'

'What had you been doing before that?'

'What had I been doing? Do you know, the *police* came and asked me that. Why on earth are you interested in little me? I asked, but they said it was just routine. Well, I'd been talking to Mary Morse about library matters. We're both on the committee: Mary because she's keen on the decency line, as you know, and me because I find it gets me the new books quicker. Well, we were talking about that on and off throughout the day, whenever we met up. I had to go round and *talk* to people, you know . . . buy things, make the right gestures. So really I was talking to all and sundry, all the time, but *when* I was talking to *who* (or should that be whom?) I really can't say. Now Mary left the tent—oh, about two-thirty or three, and after that I continued to go round . . . talked to Mrs Culpepper, I remember, and her insignificant little husband, who had the discarded toy stall —so unlike *your* husband, my dear.'

'And had you talked to Marcus that day?'

'Oh, but ye-es,' she said, summoning Li Chen for her bill. 'But much earlier. Before I went into the tent, when I was going around the games outside. Your Marcus was demonstrating his machine, and doing so well, and I said one of my silly little things—"You really should be going with the Olympic team"—something quite foolish like that. But your husband was a *man*. You've lost a treasure.' She got up, and went pink again as she remembered her mistake.

'I can't *say* how sorry I am. That I didn't remember who you were, I mean. *So* unfortunate. Say you've forgiven me. I shall dream about that tonight!'

And Lady Godetia stuffed a ten-pound note into Mr Li's hands and fled. It was clear that she was infinitely more upset by her social gaffe than by Marcus's death.

As I watched her retreating back—and it was quite a back—a voice from the next table said:

'We do seem to get encumbered with the dimmest of the upper crust in Hexton, don't we?'

I turned my head and saw that while we had been talking, Mr Horsforth had come and sat himself at the next table. Horsforth, I remembered, quite often lunched out—a perfectly sensible decision for a widower with no particular obligation to partake of the depleted and unsavoury school meals service currently provided by the County. He sat there, a glass of iced water in front of him, waiting for Li Chen to arrive with his food. On his face was that expression of fastidious superiority which was what I most disliked about him. Not that I had any inclination to fling myself to the defence of Lady Godetia.

'Yes,' I said. 'I believe there are gentry who have brains larger than a pea, but she's not among them.'

'Her husband was the same,' went on Mr Horsforth, with a sarcastic smile of reminiscence. 'Thick as two planks. He was a constant embarrassment at speech days. Since the guest speaker invariably went on about what a hopeless dullard he was at school, it was very much *de trop* for the Chairman of Governors to prove the same with every word he uttered.'

To give Mr Horsforth his due, he had never run the sort of school where it is implied that Michael Jackson is quite as commendable an object of interest as Beethoven, or that *The Thorn Birds* is the modern equivalent of Dickens. Still, at that point I was not inclined to give Mr Horsforth his due, or to let him off what I'd put the others through. If I was leaving Hexton anyway, I would not in the future be dependent on him for jobs.

'And where,' I asked, 'were you on Saturday afternoon?'

He looked at me, with a touch of granite in his eyes.

'I'd heard that you'd been going round asking questions of that kind. It's rather suspected you're intent on discovering everyone's little secrets into the bargain. I suppose it's natural, though I'm not at all sure it's wise. Or even helpful. Marcus, I should have thought, was not the sort who would go around uncovering the things people prefer to keep hidden.'

'Nevertheless,' I said, 'I should very much like to know what you were doing—let's say between three-thirty and four on Saturday afternoon.'

'Very much what I had been doing for the rest of the day, I suppose.'

'That,' I said, 'was what I never found out.'

Again that bleak look razed me.

'I rather gather,' he said, in a voice like the Isle of Arran on a wet November day, 'that you expected me to spend more time on the knick-knacks stall than I actually did. I must confess I never realized that that was expected of me.'

'You thought your duties were purely nominal? There to lend your name? Ah, well—these little misunderstandings will occur. But the question remains, since you were rarely on the stall, where were you?'

He sighed.

'It's really too childish, Mrs Kitterege, if you imagine I have some little love-nest in the town, to which I repaired stealthily from time to time during the day. I don't have some little liaison which I carry on after dark or at weekends. Headmasters really cannot do that kind of thing in their own back yards—even in these times. In fact, I wonder whether you realize what a headmaster's job has become like, these last few years. We have a government that has no belief in education—State education, at any rate—and begrudges us every penny we spend on books and equipment. I have to beg for pencils, beg for stationery, ask parents to provide things that ten years ago they and we would have taken it for granted the County would provide. And these are parents who are feeling the pinch financially themselves—frequently are actually unemployed.'

'Granted,' I said. 'I've seen this myself at school.'

'What that means is that headmasters have become compulsive beggars and button-holers: anyone with influence, anyone with anything to give, we have to be on to: Mrs X is on the County Education Committee; Mr Y is with ICI; Mrs Z is with the Social Services Department. All of them can be useful for *some* thing. That's what my life is these days. A headmaster shouldn't be a scholar, he should have a diploma in business management.'

'I'll buy that,' I said.

'I don't care greatly whether you *buy* it or not,' said Mr Horsforth, who would clearly like to have lost his temper with me (he kept his temper on a very short fuse, as a matter of policy), but felt that it was hardly the time or the place. 'It happens to be the truth.'

'So what you were doing all day was—in essence—talking to people who mattered?'

'Precisely. People who mattered to the school. People who could help preserve the threatened standards of the school . . . So if you are going around looking for secrets, you won't find any in my activities on Saturday afternoon. Try some other tack.'

He sat back, smiling complacently.

'Like drink, perhaps?' I hazarded.

He practically threw himself out of his chair at me, his face purple with rage.

'How the hell did you know about that?' he hissed.

That was an interesting question, really. It came to me pretty much the moment I said it, and I'm inclined to call it inspiration—that is, a sudden coming together of

observations and scraps of information that hitherto had
been scattered, pigeonholed in various corners of my mind.
There was that sight of the glass of water on the table—
nothing in itself, because a headmaster would be ill-advised
to drink in the middle of the school day. There was the fact
that Timothy, his son, was never on any account to be seen
in a pub—not, at least, in the Hexton area. And there was
the fact that once, long ago, when I first had a spell teaching
in his school, one of the forms had had as a nickname for
him 'The Brandy Head'. Mostly he was called the inevitable
things—Horsey, Sarky, Beaky, and suchlike—but this
group had been studying for GCE *The Power and the Glory*,
with its whisky priest, and they called him The Brandy
Head because one of the boys claimed to have seen him at
a distant rubbish tip, getting rid of a carton of brandy
bottles.

'I regard this as a serious matter,' he went on, in an
apoplectic whisper. 'Who's been talking? McPhail, I suppose. What was it? Some sort of professional confidence
between him and Marcus?'

'I assure you, doctors do not exchange professional confidences with vets. It's quite possible Marcus might have
mentioned any of Smokey's problems to Dr McPhail, but
quite impossible that McPhail should have revealed to
Marcus anything of the problems of . . . your wife, I presume?'

There was a pause while Horsforth was brought chicken
and almonds and a plate of noodles. He settled into them
moodily. I had finished my king prawns, and I demanded
another glass of Li Chen's wine-box Jugoslav Riesling.

'It was a disease with her,' he said at last, with an
expression of dyspeptic distaste on his face. 'Something
medical. Something she had inherited.' (Anything, in fact,
except a reaction to the sort of life she had, married to him.)
'She was immensely cunning in getting hold of it. I used to
wonder how she found the money to pay for it, from the

housekeeping money I gave her. Later I discovered she'd had an inheritance from an uncle that she'd told me nothing about. It was just a few hundreds, but enough. Imagine concealing a legacy, intending to spend it on drink! By the end I had to supply her—the alternative was worse. You can imagine the problems that would have been caused if anyone had found out, but by then she wouldn't have cared if the whole town knew, just so long as she got as much as she needed. I tried to persuade her to go away, to some clinic or cure, but she said what was the use? She'd just take up with it again as soon as she came home. And I knew she was right . . . You can imagine the sort of effect this had on our son, on Timothy.'

'I can imagine,' I said carefully, 'that it must have made him . . . secretive. Turned him inward, made him adept at hiding things.'

He looked at me in astonishment.

'Oh no. Not at all. You obviously don't know Timothy at all. He's a very open boy. We have a complete understanding. He has no secrets from me at all. No—I meant how strongly he took against drink, and all that . . . sordidness.'

'Ah,' I said.

'In a way that's one good thing that has come out of the whole dreadful business. He's a terribly upright boy, Timothy, and I've never had reason to be other than proud of him. Not brilliant—I'd have liked an academic career for him, naturally, but still, he's doing very well at the accountants'. He was glad when she died . . . We didn't say so to each other, but we each knew the other was glad.'

'You were spared possible embarrassment,' I said.

'We were spared watching that human degradation,' he replied, once more sharp and self-confident. 'If you've never seen anything like that, you've no cause to adopt that ironic tone. Now you know my little secret. Is it satisfying? Do you really imagine it can have anything to do with the death of Marcus? I tell you one thing: if I find that it's got around town, I'll make sure you never do a day's teaching with any Education Authority within a hundred-mile radius of this town.'

'It certainly won't get around via me,' I said, signalling to Li Chen that I wanted to pay. 'I intend to leave this place and its secrets. My only interest is in finding out who killed Marcus and why. Remember Marcus, Mr Horsforth? Remember that he was once a human being, before he became a murder case?'

He suddenly looked embarrassed.

'Yes. Of course, I should have said something. That silly woman put it out of my head. I was very sad about it— very sad indeed. He was a good influence in the town, none better. I'm afraid the murder, and all the uncertainty, put it out of my mind.'

'That's what's happened with most people,' I said sadly. 'They've forgotten Marcus, because he was murdered.'

CHAPTER 15

THE WESTONS

I was not altogether sure that it was worthwhile going to see Colonel and Mrs Weston. Marcus had always got on well with the Colonel, though he sometimes found him infuriatingly slow and non-committal (Marcus, be it said, being far from fast or committal himself). The Colonel had been right behind Marcus in his fight for charity and sanity in the parish of St Edward the Confessor, and Mrs Weston had not joined forces to any noticeable extent with the harpies of Hexton. The police, surely, would have got out of the Westons all there was to be got?

On the other hand, they were the parents of Fiona, whose doings still intrigued me (on a personal, gossipy, level, rather than as anything that might be of relevance). And they were among the last, presumably, to have seen Marcus alive, and simply on those grounds it seemed foolish to neglect them. I rang up Nancy Weston and (in effect) invited myself round for four-fifteen the next day. She promised me muffins if it was cool, which was a good start.

It was cool—one of the few cool days that summer— when I made my way down St Joseph's Wynd, in the direction of their house. I hoped the muffins would be good. Through a gap in the street, over the wall of a little garden path, I could see their house. I paused in my progress as I saw the front door open, and I watched as Timothy and Fiona came out. What was this? The young ones making their escape because they knew an oldie was coming to tea? Or was it something very different—were they coming to meet me, to waylay me before I could get there? Yes—they were turning in the direction they knew I would arrive from.

I paused a little longer, and as soon as they began along the road I knew there was something odd about them. They had changed their performance. This new act was called Temporary Interruption to Love's Young Dream. Or perhaps, if they had been painted by a nineteenth-century painter, The Falling-Out. Hands were not held, and they mooched along at least a foot apart, discontent written all over the set of their faces, tension written on the set of their shoulders. Timothy kicked a soft-drink can left in the gutter; Fiona gazed at the gables of houses and pouted. Doubtless already they had been observed from behind the curtains of front rooms; perhaps already telephone lines were singing as the Hexton information service ('You know I'm not one to gossip, but do you know what I've just seen?') spread the news through the town and the surrounding farms and cottages.

'Well,' I said, as we met at the corner, just as they had intended we should. 'This makes a change.'

Heads kept shaded from observers, they smiled, nervously and conspiratorially.

'It's a new stage in the affair,' said Fiona.

'I think you're very wise. What you had was a Second Couple routine. It would never have sustained a whole play.'

'Actually,' said Timothy, 'we're keeping our options open, but we're thinking of making this The Beginning of the End.'

'Really? I should have thought with Rows and Reconciliations this was a show that could have run and run.'

'Well, it's got to end some time, hasn't it? And if we break up, I can borrow Dad's car and go off on long, moody drives at weekends. And Fiona can go and stay with friends, or *say* that's what she's doing, to take her mind off things. We can spin it out for a bit, and it might prove even better than what we've got going now. We wouldn't need to see each other so much, for example.'

'What we came along for,' said Fiona, 'was to make sure you were not thinking of telling. That way we know all our options are open.'

'No, I certainly wasn't thinking of telling,' I said. 'Anyone who fights the Hexton code has my general sympathy. On the other hand, I would rather like to know what I'm not telling. What precisely, I mean, has all this been a cover for?'

'But we thought you *knew*!'

'Not entirely,' I said. 'It was more in the way of a lucky shot in the dark.'

'Well, that *is* rather rotten of you,' said Fiona. But the two of them looked at each other conspiratorially.

'Well?' I said, waiting.

'Well,' said Timothy, 'we're both of us, in a way, reacting against Hexton, if you see what I mean.'

'Quite,' I said. 'I've already said that, and it was pretty predictable. What I wanted to know was the precise form your reactions were taking.'

'Fiona, you see, has this friend. Lover. He works on a fairground—travels all the seaside places in the North during the summer, jobs with a circus during the winter. Sort of gipsy bloke, you know.'

'Madly exciting,' said Fiona, flashing her eyes from beneath her shaded head. 'Sort of exotic—foreign, sweaty, and *not* like anything I've ever known. Of course, in the nature of things it's not likely to be more than a *fling* . . .'

'You disappoint me. Do you mean you're going to land up eventually with a young stockbroker type? Pinstripes and fast cars and the Young Conservatives' Ball?'

'Well, I suppose it *may* come to that. Mummy is very persistent, in her soft kind of way, and of course I like my comforts. Love in a caravan can be exciting—Golly! I never *knew* how exciting caravans could be!—but you wouldn't want it when you're forty-five, I shouldn't imagine. But at least I'll have the memory, won't I? And if it doesn't by any chance fizzle out naturally, well, I'll let it dawn on Mummy and Daddy lightly . . . And Timothy, of course, has what one might call a *tendresse*.'

'An attachment,' said Timothy. 'You make it sound so Barbara Cartland. An attachment. I met him at this pub in Darlington that I . . . we go to. He's a major at the barracks. I think I represent something he can't find among the recruits.'

'I can imagine. I suppose he himself is minor public school, with a Profile?'

'Something like that,' admitted Timothy.

'Well, in the nature of things you're going to have to say something to your father about *that*.'

'Oh, do you think so? My idea was just to cover it up—my tastes, I mean—until I'm financially independent. That won't be long now. Then I can get a flat somewhere or other, and leave the tyrannical old shit. He killed my mother, you know.'

'By driving her to drink?'

'Exactly. It was drink or suicide for her. He left her no room for any personality of her own. When she'd finally died, I looked at him, over her body, to say: *I know*. And he . . . well, you know what he is . . . he wilfully misunderstood. What line he cares to take after I move out about my tastes, if he hears of them, I don't much care. I doubt I'll want to see anything much of him. I'll have a life of my own at last.'

It struck me that Timothy and Fiona's rebellions against the stifling conventions of Hexton were of a distinctly cool and calculating nature. Perhaps it was in the nature of a Hexton upbringing that that should be so. Certainly there seemed to be no burning of bridges for these two: play safe until you're firmly on the opposite shore. I had a fair degree of sympathy for Timothy, because I knew enough about the nature of his father to see what an intolerable home life he must have had. Fiona's rebellion was against a pair whom I had always regarded as reasonably amiable old fuddies, but I did have to admit that I knew nothing at all about the sort of home life they might have created for her.

'You will keep the secret for a bit, won't you?' Fiona said, wheedling, with something of a return to her old ingénue manner. 'I mean, it will be so much better if it comes out *ever* so gradually . . . so that they wonder, then they have doubts, then they worry, and so on—*you* know.'

I assured her that I had no interest in doing an 'I thought you ought to know' to her parents, and they went off towards town, resuming quite without effort their Broken Blossoms routine. When I got to the Westons it was clear that the process of wondering had begun already. From behind the curtains of the front room Mrs Weston's eyes were following them, heavy with maternal worry. When she opened the front door, she watched them as they turned towards the town centre, and said:

'I really don't know what's got into those two.'

'Lovers' tiff, I expect,' I said, comfortably.

'You noticed? It's so *unlike* them. Always so wrapped up

in each other, it's been a joy to watch them.'

Positively puke-making, in my view, but there's no accounting for tastes, particularly maternal ones.

'One never actually marries one's first love, not if one is wise,' I said. It was a most unpopular thing to say.

'You don't mean you thought that the quarrel was *that* serious, did you?' Mrs Weston's face was all screwed up with anguish at the thought. 'Oh, I do hope not. Such a *nice* boy. So suitable. Nothing special *so*cially, of course, but so pleasant and respectful, so nice-looking, so prese*nt*able . . . I really have set my heart on their getting married.'

I looked at her as she ushered me towards their little drawing-room. This, I thought, was the New Snobbery. You didn't worry any more about family, about daddy's income, or the size of the ancestral seat; you worried about how he would look in the wedding photographs, about presentability, about glossy surfaces. Timothy's appeal for her was that you could take him anywhere. I had to admit that Mrs Weston seemed a much sillier woman than I had thought, and the New Snobbery quite as unattractive as the old.

You had to hand it to Fiona, though: she really did seem to have gone the whole hog with her boyfriend. A gipsy circus-hand seemed to represent the diametrical opposite of every standard that Mrs Weston held most dear. He was the sort of man you could take nowhere. Exciting, I imagined, for Fiona.

In the drawing-room Colonel Weston was sitting in his armchair, presiding over a silver-covered dish and the usual Hexton array of flowery china. He floundered to his feet and made various inarticulate noises of commiseration, then sank down again like a sea creature that is only happy on the ocean bed.

Mrs Weston presided fluffily, though I could see that the worry about Fiona and Timothy was still at the back of her mind. The muffins were shop-y, which was disappointing, but warmth and butteriness go quite a way, and I tucked into them.

We talked for a bit about neutral things. Father Battersby's first service had been a great success: all the odds and bobs of a High Church celebration had gone down extremely well, rather like suddenly acquiring a colour television after you've only been used to black and white. According to Colonel Weston several people had said afterwards that it was nice to have something to look at, and something to smell, so that you weren't 'thrown in on yourself', as one member of the congregation expressed it. Personally Father Battersby was going down very well, though his habit of making tactless remarks had not quite left him: he had referred to his intention of doing something 'when Mrs Primp is out of the way', but he had done so to one of the few local people to regret her departure—her dressmaker, if you'll believe she had one.

'Anyway,' said Weston, with traditional military gruffness, 'the more he gets to know people, the less he'll make mistakes like that—eh? And poor old Thyrza left yesterday, you know.'

'Of course—Wednesday,' I said.

'It's like the end of an era,' said Mrs Weston pensively. She really was a very silly woman.

'That, at any rate, is what she would like people to feel,' I said. 'With Mary Morse waiting in the wings to take over, unasked and unwanted, the position of honorary vicar's wife, I doubt if we shall notice any difference. Unless Father Battersby puts up a fight against her pretensions, and nips them in the bud.'

'Rather think he will,' said Colonel Weston. 'Wouldn't be surprised if he didn't enjoy a scrap. Born fighter—eh?'

'Maybe,' I said. 'Anyway, not a smoother over, like Marcus. It was about Marcus that I wanted to talk.'

They both shifted uneasily in their seats, but then everyone I spoke to did that. I thought we'd got *that* disagreeable topic out of the way, they all seemed to want to say.

'Of course, my dear,' said Nancy Weston, looking slightly abstracted. 'But I really don't see what we can tell you.'

'Well, for a start, you were both among the last to see him alive.'

'Well, yes, we were that. But there really wasn't anything special about that. I mean, he just went off. As we told the Superintendent, it was time for us to take over, and we did so. Then Marcus just went off.'

'Quickly?'

'Yes, he was walking fairly fast.'

'After someone?'

'The Superintendent asked that. But we just didn't notice, did we, Frank? We were checking the equipment, and I was seeing to the cash box, and then we had a customer, so we simply didn't notice. One minute he was there with us, the next he was gone.'

'So you didn't notice anything special about him?'

'No, I don't think so, did we, dear?'

'Same as usual—sure of it.'

'He didn't *say* anything unusual?'

'No, really, dear: we'd have told the police if he had, naturally.'

'Did you take over from him on the Test Your Strength game several times in the course of the day?'

'Oh yes. He had a tea-break about twelve. That was just twenty minutes or so, and he collected a cup and went down to the river with his pipe. Then he had another break—when was it, dear?—round about two. He went into the tent: probably you saw him?'

'Yes, I did. So you saw him fairly often, whenever you took over from him, or he took over from you. Was he always his usual self when you talked to him? Nothing upsetting him, or anything?'

'I *think* so—don't you, dear?'

'There was that time—' began Colonel Weston in his usual inarticulate way.

'When, dear?'

'After he'd been in the tent. You remember.'

'Oh yes. I don't *think* that was anything, dear. It was after that second spell off, when you saw him. And when he came back he did seem very thoughtful—sort of preoccupied. And Frank said—what did you say, dear?'

'Don't remember exactly. Thought something had gone wrong in the tent. Thought one of those damned women— beg y'pardon, m'dear—thought one of those women must have had a slanging match with Father B, or something. So I said, "All Quiet on the Western Front?" or something of the sort. And he said, "Oh yes, perfectly quiet. Everything going very nicely indeed."'

'Was that all?'

'I think so. I said, "No need for us to do anything, then?" and he replied: "No need at all" . . . No, wait, I lie. He said: "No need to do anything at all. Not about that."'

'He didn't explain?'

'No. He was still a bit quiet and thoughtful, so we drifted off, didn't we, Nance, saying we'd be back in good time to take over again at three-thirty.'

I sat in a trance, and let them talk on. Mrs Weston was very good at talking on—covering over, she thought, any little social awkwardnesses. I was thinking over those words: 'Not about that.' I was remembering back to that scene in the tent, the last time I had seen Marcus alive, the last time I had talked to him. How casual, brusque, unthinking I had been—I had thought about that often since. We had held hands under the table, I remembered, but then I had left with hardly a goodbye. But what had we talked about, what had been going on around us?

I conjured up pictures, scraps of conversation—straining my mind back through the five days of grief since it had happened. What had I seen in those minutes, what had I heard? And yet, of course, what I had seen was not necessarily what Marcus had seen. He was a good five inches taller than me. I remembered that I had not noticed until late in the afternoon that Howard Culpepper had a stall two or three down from mine. On the other hand, probably what Marcus had *heard* must have been pretty much what I myself heard.

I pulled myself together with a start. Nancy Weston was talking to me.

'I'm sorry,' I said.

'Not at all, dear. I was just saying that I'd heard you were intending to leave Hexton.'

'Yes,' I said. 'Oh yes. I think so.'

'Damned shame,' said Colonel Weston. 'After all you and Marcus have done for the place.'

Only a man of Colonel Weston's gallantry could have included me in that sentence.

'It's understandable you should want to get away,' said Mrs Weston. 'Where will you go?'

'I really haven't thought. I haven't had time to find out what money there will be, let alone think about looking for a job. With the job situation at the moment, I should think genteel poverty and genteel unemployment are likely to be my lot, but I'll investigate one or two possibilities. I suppose first I'll go and stay with Mother.'

'That's nice,' said Nancy Weston in her wet way. 'She's a widow, isn't she? You'll be company for each other.'

'For a time, I suppose. But we both have our own ways, and two generations in the same house never really works, does it?'

'She's quite an old lady?'

'Yes, indeed. I was a youngest child. She's getting rather forgetful, and living mostly in the past. Things have changed too much for her in recent years, and she doesn't like it. When I tell her the price of anything she asks: "What's that in real money?" Within a week or two of my going back she'll be telling me to eat up my nice greens. No, it won't work for very long . . .'

Mrs Weston was beginning to say something anodyne, when suddenly something clicked. Just as something had at Mary's, but this was a definite click—confusing but definite. A connection. Yet what on earth could the connection mean? I stood up.

'I'm sorry. I've just thought of something—something rather important. I think I'd better be getting home.'

And that's what I did, leaving three muffins congealing in their own butter. I said my farewells to the Westons, had no impulse to satisfy the wondering expression on Nancy Weston's face, and walked rapidly up and down the wynds of Hexton, thinking furiously, seeing nobody and nothing, until I arrived home—all the time wondering what on earth could come of that click, what conceivable relevance it could have.

CHAPTER 16

SEEING THE LIGHT

By the oddest of coincidences I received a further less confusing revelation soon after I got home. When I opened the door, Jasper behaved, as usual, as if I had left him without food and water to go on a fortnight's package tour, so as always I gave way to the guilt feelings he intends to inspire and allowed him a few throws of the ball in the garden. When we both got tired of that, I went into the sitting-room and turned on the television. Marcus used to think against a background of music, I do it against a background of television. He frequently had only the vaguest of ideas what he had been listening to ('Was it Mozart? Yes, I'm sure it was Mozart,' he would say, when I knew it had been Vaughan Williams), and similarly quiz game or soap opera glided slippily from one side of my mind to the other and out, without leaving any distinct memory (which is perhaps the idea behind them).

Today, however, the first image to come up on the screen seized my mind. It was the five-forty news, and as usual the first item was the miners' strike—for the country was going through one of its regular large-scale industrial upheavals. There was uproar coming from the set, as there had been the night before, and would be the night after: there were pictures of running battles, as overweight thugs hurled whatever came to hand at the police, and police did thorough jobs with their truncheons whenever they thought (wrongly) that they were out of sight of a television camera. It was a depressing spectacle, and I was about to switch off when the picture changed to one of an official of the South Yorkshire Miners' Executive—a white collar spokesman, though he didn't in fact wear a white collar, or a tie. He immediately launched into the familiar routine: 'Our members, subjected to extreme police violence and intimidation, launched a limited retaliatory action . . . reminiscent of a Fascist dictatorship . . . police state . . . rights of the working people of this country to pursue traditional trade union picketing in a peaceful manner . . .'

It was done with a Pecksniffian relish, a delighted going-through-the-motions, that did not want or expect to be believed. And the person going through the motions was Mary Morse's brother John. No doubt about it. The beard did not disguise the sly, resentful face; the relish might have been directed, through the camera, at Mary, at her dead mother, and at the whole edifice of Morsism.

No question now why Mary wanted to keep quiet about her younger brother. Not bankruptcy or lunacy, but militant trade unionism, more shameful than either, and more hideously culpable in Hexton's eyes, because embraced quite voluntarily. I resolved on the morrow to spread myself through town, asking everyone: 'Did you see Mary's brother on the telly last night? Wasn't he good?'

Or would I, perhaps, have something still more pressing to do on the morrow?

I fed Jasper, got something—anything—marked 'For One' out of the freezer, then settled down with a little notebook on the sofa. Only by writing things down could I bring some sort of order to the confusion. Because, though I was learning things, though I was remembering things, still the various pieces did not seem to be fitting into the same jigsaw. I had gone at the case with too many preconceptions. On the one hand there was the jigsaw labelled 'Hexton—' the public and private faces of the town, its dated customs, its mealy-mouthed morality, its collapsing series of façades. On the other hand, there seemed to be another jigsaw . . .

I took my pen, and on a blank sheet of paper wrote:

Change

Jasper was restive, and managing to throw balls for himself. He had jumped over and across me several times before I had thought through the implications of that one word. When I had, I pondered again, and wrote down the word:

Priest

This provoked less thought, and I just added 'check' beside it, before writing:

Hexton

After a time I wrote 'check too' by this word, and wrote a last entry that I thought rather interesting:

Nonsense language?

It was not, I had to conclude, much. It was certainly not,

in police language, a 'case'. Nevertheless, I was sure that it was in some sense the answer. I went into the kitchen to peel some potatoes, and to heat up the frozen 'For One' dish. It turned out to be a peculiarly nasty braised something-or-other that I had made long ago, before I knew better than to try out *The Times*'s cookery correspondent's recipes. It didn't matter. After the first mouthful I didn't really notice what I was eating. I was too preoccupied with thinking the thing through, with filling in the areas around the few clues and indications I had gathered together in my mind. When I had finished my meal, and washed out the taste with a glass of wine, I got on the phone to the Superintendent.

The Superintendent, though I haven't mentioned it, had been in constant touch with me over the case, ringing me once and sometimes twice a day. I haven't mentioned it because he rarely told me anything of any great moment. I was, after all, a suspect, and would remain one until somebody was arrested. So I heard how many tourists the police had interviewed, how they were attempting to establish the precise doings and whereabouts of many people (including, no doubt, me, though he didn't say so) at the relevant period of the afternoon, how the army had put the drunken lout who threw Marcus's body into the river on a charge, and so on. I never got any sense that he was any forrader, and I don't think he did either.

'I sometimes think,' he had said to me the day before, 'that this murder was done on the spur of the moment, and it was pure luck that there was no one around to see it.'

'That's what Father Battersby thinks,' I said.

'That sort of murder is the very devil to solve, especially if the chap keeps his head afterwards.'

'Or her head,' I had said.

Now I got on to him and explained some of the things I had been thinking of, the way some little, unnoticed things had begun to form a pattern in my mind. He was sympathetic, but quiet—very quiet. I presumed he was unimpressed.

'What you have there is a motive, not a case,' he said.

'I realize that. I was hoping that establishing the motive might be the first step to establishing the case.'

'Certainly there are things there we could check up on—things we would want to check up on before we did anything at all in the way of confrontation. Basically, what we would be depending on would be the suspect breaking down. A chancy thing, that. The suspect clearly hasn't broken down so far.'

'What I was wondering,' I said, 'was whether I might not be more likely to effect the breaking-down than you. The personal touch, rather than the majesty of the law.'

Well, we talked about this for some time, and the Super did not greatly like it, but as he said: he could not dictate to me who I could see and who I could not see. And as I said, I had a fair bit to do before I would be ready. Finally he said he would have a man keeping an eye on me all the next day, and he would call for a second, to police both front and back doors, any time I should go into a house other than my own. I said that was all right by me. I had not, to tell you the truth, given much thought to my own safety, probably because I was still in the numbness of the newly-bereaved, taking each day as it came. 'Tomorrow is the first day of the rest of your life' is no doubt a fine inspirational text for some, but not for those for whom the rest of their lives yawns empty and lonely compared with what had gone before. I was not very interested in the rest of my life, so I didn't greatly care about my own safety.

But I did very much want to get the murderer of Marcus.

CHAPTER 17

FINAL ACCOUNTS

The next day I took Jasper for his walk very early on. We went to the meadows—the first time I had been there since the day of the fête. There was nobody around on them, except the police constable who was keeping an eye on me from a distance. Jasper was delighted with his company, and kept running up to him, wagging his tail, and trying to persuade him to throw balls. The young man looked embarrassed, as if he were a spy whose cover had been blown.

If he has an early walk, Jasper is usually all right until tea-time. I didn't know how long things were likely to take that day. When I got in I had a cup of coffee, did some checking in Marcus's records, and planned things out. It should look as like a normal day as possible, I thought. I put some library books in my shopping-bag and sallied forth.

People were getting used to seeing me in the streets by now. They had decided it was all right just to nod and pass on. When I went into the shops, though, the other shoppers felt trapped. Even if it was only a supermarket, they felt our trolleys might meet round a corner and they be compelled to make some unorthodox gesture. That morning I went into Mr Hussein's to get some of his pâté, and said brightly to the other waiting souls:

'Did you see Mary Morse's brother on television last night?'

No, they all nodded dumbly.

'Oh yes. The NUM spokesman for the miners at Scunthorpe. He was *so* articulate. Mary must be awfully proud.'

And I smiled wickedly. *She's* back to her normal bitch form, the other shoppers thought, or some Hexton formulation that meant the same thing. But I'm sure they went away and passed it on. In Hexton that is the sort of thing that is bound to be passed on.

Then I went to the library. It is a rather damp, dreary building on the outskirts of the old town, and a general air of Mary Morse hangs over it. Since the sort of middle-brow, middle-class, middle-IQ novel that is approved of here is not produced much these days, they will buy almost anything you specially order, but they do so with an air of 'Are you *sure* this is the sort of thing you want to read?' The librarians are scraps of gentility who look as if they had been personally screened by Thyrza Primp, as very probably they had. They made no comment on my un-Hexton reappearance in the first week of widowhood, merely compressing their lips and handing me my cards. They noticed me, though—noticed that I didn't do my usual thing of flipping through the books on the 'Recently Returned' trolley, in the faint hope of finding a vintage Christie I hadn't read, or the new Fay Weldon. Instead I went straight along to the super-dreary reference section—roped off, for some reason, from the rest—and settled myself down at a table. 'What on earth is she doing?' I could almost hear them asking each other. The reference library is quite unfrequented as a rule, like the mausoleum of a once-proud family that has died out. I was rather surprised to find that it had what I wanted. 'She's at the dictionaries!' I could imagine the librarians saying in their bewilderment. 'The foreign dictionaries! Do you think she's doing crosswords to while away the time?' When I left I just grabbed a volume from the shelves to take out. The librarians looked at me through narrowed slits of eyes, and when I got outside I found out why. The book was called *It Shouldn't Happen to a Vet*.

The policeman was loitering around in a conspicuous fashion when I came out into the street again. He followed me at a respectful distance as I made my way through town again, and up to Mrs Nielson's. As usual, I heard Gustave's staccato yap, and Gwen Nielson calming him down: '*There's a marvellous watch-dog! There's a clever fellow! Will my boy go into the kitchen while Mumsie sees who it is?*'

When she came to the door she smiled deprecatingly as the hail of barks continued from inside the house.

'Sorry about him. He'll be all right when he knows it's you. Come in. Is it too late for morning coffee?'

'Actually, I've had more than my fair share of morning coffee and afternoon tea recently. I just wanted a bit of help, and I don't need anything to go with it.'

'Right. Here—Gustave, you daft animal. Got who it is? Right? Now, out you go and have a sniff around the garden!'

And she heaved him out of the back door and led me through into the sitting-room.

'Well, now: how are you getting on?'

'Not bad, not bad. I'm finding out a variety of delectable little secrets, some of which I may tell you, some of which I cannot. Did you know, for example, that one of Mary's brothers is helping to organize the miners' strike?'

'No!'

'But he is! No great credit to my detective ability that I found it out. He happened to be on television a day or two after I had studied his picture in Mary's sitting-room. I expect most of Hexton's forgotten what he looks like by now. Imagine—a Marxist Morse! Worse than a blasphemous Bishop! No wonder they've kept quiet about him, and Mary has more or less turned his picture to the wall.'

'I presume you're telling everyone?'

'What do you think? About some of the other things I have to be a little more circumspect ... But that wasn't really what I came to talk about today. I have found out one or two things, things that I think are relevant, and what I'm trying to do now is recreate what Marcus saw and heard during the last hour or two of his life. Now, you remember when he came along to talk to me by my stall, just before we two went off for lunch?'

'Yes. We were waiting for Mr Horsforth to turn up.'

'That's it. Hexton's Godot he was, wasn't he? Now, it occurs to me that what Marcus saw when he was standing by my stall wasn't necessarily what I saw. He was much taller than I, after all, and I was hemmed in behind my stall, looking straight over to you, and the people at stalls on either side of you. Now Marcus was much freer, and could look all around. I thought that you, being opposite, might have seen things that I *wouldn't* have seen, but that Marcus *would*.'

'Well, of course I could see the stalls on your side of the aisle—would you call it an aisle? There was Mrs Slackbridge on the one side, Mr Turnhill on the other. Those you would have seen yourself. Then, further down—'

'Yes?'

'On one side there was Mrs Fox with the clothing exchange, on the other, Howard Culpepper with the toys.'

'That's right, though in fact I didn't notice Howard until very late in the day.'

'Does one ever? He had a pile of toys and jigsaws and games, and they cost practically nothing, and the children were supposed to be able to bring their old ones along and swap them, though hardly any of them did, that I saw.'

'He didn't do good business?'

'I don't think so. Not having any children, he doesn't seem to have much of a touch with them. Talks down rather, and puts on false ho-ho chuckles. He didn't seem to go down well at all. I really don't know how people get chosen for these jobs. Look at me: I can tell a runny jam from a firm one, but I don't even like the stuff, and I couldn't for the life of me *make* a jar.'

'Quite apart from the fact that, having lived abroad for so long, you had trouble giving the right change, didn't you?'

'Yes, I . . . I can't imagine what makes you think I've lived abroad.'

There was silence in the room, and I let it tick on. Suddenly, seated deep in her capacious leather chair of Scandinavian design, she looked very small. I noticed her fingers were tearing away at a little lace handkerchief in her lap. When she spoke I sensed defeat already in her voice.

'I come from down South. My husband was a doctor . . . a hospital doctor down South.'

'No doubt the police could check that quite easily. For myself, I'm quite sure without checking that it's not true. The first time I spoke to you properly, you had just given Mr Hussein at the delicatessen the wrong money. As Marcus stood with me that last time, people were coming away from your stall complaining that you'd given them the wrong change. Yet you give the impression of being a very competent person generally—capable, very much in control. There have been a lot of changes in the currency over the last decade or so, haven't there? Decimalization, the new coins. But we've all caught up with them by now, those of us who've lived through the changes. The only people who get it wrong nowadays are the very old, and people who've been out of the country for a long time.'

'I never was any good at mathematics.'

'You don't need to be good these days. It's a perfectly simple currency. And you did a bit of simple mathematics perfectly competently while we were sitting outside having our lunch on the day of the fête. It was not mathematics that defeated you, it was the new coins. You were making the sort of mistakes that we all made in the early days of decimal coinage: the old two-shilling piece became ten pence, but we made it *twenty*, because we had the *two* firmly in our minds. Then there are all the completely new coins that have come in recently, too. And there were other things . . .'

I was interrupted by a crescendo of barking from the back garden.

'The second policeman taking up position,' I said significantly.

She started up from her lethargy.

'You can't think I'd—?'

'Why not? You've done it before.'

Slowly, miserably, knowing its significance, she said:

'It's because I have done it before that I could never do it again. You can't know the feeling—'

'I don't want to know the feeling,' I interrupted. 'Let's keep feelings out of this. I don't think I'm likely to feel sympathy.'

She drew back as it stung. I looked at her, crouched there, unutterably miserable and defeated, like a worn-out dish-rag. This was the confident, capable woman who had come to Hexton. I could not feel pity, however, only a horrible curiosity. I went on inexorably:

'There were other things which, when I thought about it, set you apart. Little things, all of them, but when I put them together in my mind they added up: they suggested to me that you had been out of the country for some time. You always, whenever you spoke of them, referred to Father Battersby and Walter Primp as "priests". Perfectly all right, of course, but a middle-class person from the South, like you or me, almost always refers to his Church of England minister as a "clergyman" or a "vicar". There is something ever-so-slightly Catholic about priest, and something Mary Morse said reminded me of that. Yet you never once used those other words. I thought at first that you must have lived in a Catholic country, but that wasn't what your name suggested. It's perfectly common in England, of course, but it reminded me of Birgit Nilsson, the singer. I wondered if you hadn't simply Anglicized your real name. And I went to a Swedish dictionary in the library and found out that a clergyman is a *präst* in Swedish. So it was a natural thing to do, if you were used to talking Swedish. If the police were to ask to see any official documents about you—your driving licence, or whatever—I think they would find that your name really is Mrs Nilsson.'

The miserable object in the chair nodded.

'Similarly with Hexton. We might, in England, think of some kind of spell when we hear the word "hex", but we don't use it for a witch. When you said you thought Hexton meant "town of the witches" you were very embarrassed, not because you'd made a *faux pas*, but because you'd revealed special knowledge: *häxa* is the Swedish for "witch". And the final thing—the thing that might have given me a clue earlier—was the little boy.'

'Yes. I made a fool of myself there.'

'He was lost and crying, and you comforted him, and I assumed you were talking nonsense language to him. But of course, if you've lived abroad, I imagine that, whatever language you talk to adults, you *have* to speak the native language to small children. It would come to be instinctive. You were talking to him in Swedish.'

She nodded.

'And Marcus was by, was nearer you, and could hear better. Nonsense language for a toddler never really sounds like an actual language. And Marcus, I suspect, had noticed something before?'

She made no reply. Then suddenly she got up, went out to the kitchen, and let Gustave in by the back door. When she came back, Gustave jumped up into her lap, and she crooned over him.

'There, my precious. It's all right. Nothing to worry his clever little head about. Have a snooze on Mummy's lap ... Yes, Marcus had been behind me one day in the tobacconist's. I asked for two packets of Benson and Hedges. He shot me a look, one that I just didn't understand. I started to listen to people, and they all asked for "twenty" or "forty" of whatever they smoked. If I had been a non-smoker, Marcus possibly wouldn't have been surprised: I just wasn't used to asking for cigarettes. But he'd seen me smoking at your party for Father Battersby. In fact, I took up smoking after I went to Sweden, when my marriage started to go wrong, so naturally I asked for them in the Swedish way . . . *There*, my lovely boy. Mother's all right. Calm down, there's a lovely boy.'

'There's another thing I should have noticed,' I said, harshly. 'People who talk soppy to their dogs almost always do it in public as well as in private. As a vet's wife I'd registered that. But you did it in private, and adopted a brisk, no-nonsense approach in public. It just didn't come together. I should have realized that this all came back to Gustave.'

'Gustaf. After the king.'

'To Gustaf. And to Marcus not as churchwarden, but as vet.'

She continued crooning over him, lovingly, weeping as she stroked him, and then wiped her eyes with the torn handkerchief she had been clutching in her fist.

'I married twenty-five years ago. His name was Erik, and he was studying medicine here. Quite a lot of Scandinavians do. He was tall and fair and slim, and had the most beautiful light blue eyes I had ever seen. I didn't see that they were cold. Perhaps they weren't, then. When he graduated, we went back to Sweden, to Umeå, in the North. Lovely in summer—cold beyond belief in winter, the long, long winters. Erik got a post in the hospital. Eventually, when no children came, I went to work in the hospital too. I had trained as a nurse here, that was how we met. We talked about adopting children: there were Korean ones, and Vietnamese that were available. But he always said it would not be the same. I think at heart he was a racist. Many Scandinavians are. He let me have a dog, though. He did let me have a dog.'

She stroked Gustave, as he slept the sleep of the ignorant in her lap.

'Erik was ambitious. He wanted to get on. Umeå was

just a starting-place for him. He wanted to move down to Stockholm, or Göteborg. But he didn't get on. I think perhaps he wasn't as good as he thought he was. That was why he'd had to come to England for his training. He hadn't quite managed to get the right grades in Sweden. And he put people's backs up too. He was very cold, bitter, sarcastic —and this grew and grew. Because he thought he wasn't appreciated. I didn't have much to do with him at the hospital, but I had to cope with him at home. He got colder and colder, more and more withdrawn. Eventually there was—nothing. You know?'

'No,' I said. 'I don't.'

She glanced up at me, and then looked hurriedly down.

'When my old dog died, I mourned her, but she was nearly fifteen, and she died naturally, and I'd loved her and given her a good life. After my people died, I never used even to come back to Britain on holiday, because I couldn't take her with me. Erik said we shouldn't have another dog. He said he was fed up with the noise and the smell, and the problems when she was on heat . . . By then things were pretty bad between us . . . I just went out and bought Gustaf . . . He was the only thing I had—the only company. You'll never have known what it's like when an animal's the *only* thing one has. He was everything to me. Erik, you see, became . . . manic. It's the only way to describe it. In the end he dimly saw it himself. He went into an institution, voluntarily. I visited him there, but he was like someone I'd never known . . . Then one night he . . . took something.'

In the silence she added drearily:

'I was very glad.'

She bent to whisper secret nothings in Gustaf's ear.

'There was nothing to keep me in Sweden. I wanted to get away from that cold place. My widow's pension was very good, because of Erik's job. It would go even further in England. But there was Gustaf, and those *cruel* quarantine laws. Six months! Six months in a kennel!' Her face lit up with a momentary passion, as it had not done when she told me about her marriage. 'I do think it's cruel! *And* silly! No other nation thinks it necessary. They all accept the anti-rabies injection. Why can't Britain do the same? And even if it's necessary for animals from Italy or Portugal and places like that, it *can't* be necessary for Swedish ones. The country's a damned sight cleaner and more health-conscious than Britain!'

'Marcus thought it necessary,' I said. 'He felt strongly about keeping out rabies. He used often to marvel at the silliness of people who tried to evade the quarantine regulations.'

'Yes. Yes, I found out he felt like that . . . Anyway, there was this boy, this boy who lived next door. He was a bit rough, but nice, and rather in rebellion against all those dour, formal Swedes. You've no idea how punctilious Swedes can be, and he was a relief, and he came and talked often, when he was home. He was a sailor—he'd been in everything: merchant shipping, cruise ships, fishing-boats, the lot. One day he was round in my kitchen, and we were talking and laughing, and I was saying how I wanted, *how* I wanted, to get away, but that I couldn't bear the thought of putting Gustaf in a kennel for six months. It would have been like a betrayal—after all he'd been to me in those terrible last years of marriage. I knew people who'd had their animals in quarantine, you see. One of them said to me: "You get a dog back at the end, but it's not the same dog. Not your dog." I couldn't have borne it.'

'I think that's nonsense,' I said briskly. 'Animals adapt much more readily than we imagine.'

'Not all animals,' she said, almost fiercely. '*You* wouldn't have, would you, my precious? My angel . . . So that's what we did. He had all the necessary contacts, of course. I sold the house, and arranged to have the furniture sent into storage in England. Then I took Gustaf across into Norway, to Bodø, and this boy had arranged with a Norwegian fishing-boat skipper to smuggle him on board. Then I flew to England, bought a car, and drove up to the West coast of Scotland, where I was to pick him up. It all went so wonderfully smoothly. It was worth every penny I paid. Then Gustaf and I drove down into Yorkshire, looking for somewhere to live. Yorkshire was nice, and far from Dorset, where I was brought up. It had always been one of my favourite counties. After Umeå even the Shetlands wouldn't have seemed bleak. I looked for a house I could move into almost immediately, and we found one here. I couldn't believe everything could have gone so well.'

'But you still had to be very careful,' I said. 'I looked through the records this morning. I notice that you never used Marcus as a vet, though you pretended to me that you had.'

'No, I didn't. Just to be on the safe side. The only time Gustaf needed one, I went into Darlington. There was just the possibility of awkward questions. Of course I should have told people here that I was from Sweden, but that I'd been in the country for more than six months—staying with relatives, for example. But I was afraid to bring the idea of abroad into things at all. Then I soon found I was making mistakes—the sort of mistakes that people do make who've been out of the country for a long time. Not big, vital mistakes, as a rule, but silly little mistakes that mount up and give them away, like crossing the figure seven. Often I didn't even know I'd made them—as with "priest", or asking for "packets" of cigarettes. And that was even more frightening than if I'd realized what I'd done. I should never have accepted the invitation to your place, since Marcus was really the main danger to me. I tried to withdraw from the fête, saying I wanted to go on holiday, but you know what a frightful bully Franchita is. My instinct, when I realized I was making mistakes, was to lie as low as possible till I'd been in the country six months—then I thought nobody would worry too much. They would punish *me*, but they wouldn't . . . do anything to Gustaf. But I had to do the fête. Normally I'm quite a cool person on the surface. I've been a ward sister in a hospital, after all, so I've had to be. But sometimes the calm, efficient surface covers . . . panic! Flap! It was like that with Marcus, standing there by your stall as he did, watching everything. I started giving wrong change. That poor child was crying its heart out—I love children—and I spoke to him in *Swedish*! It was so natural. But with Marcus there!'

'And he realized, did he?'

'Oh yes. He realized. When I'd sold out, I packed up for the day and started off home. I went the long way round, by Castle Walk, to give Gustaf an extra run. He'd been such an *angel* all day, hadn't you, my bestest boy? And then I heard footsteps, coming up fast behind me. It was Marcus. And he called my name, and I stopped, and he caught up with me and came right out with it at once. He said: "Mrs Nielson, how long have you been living in this country?"'

There was silence in the room. I thought about poor Marcus, sailing unawares and fearless to his stupid, unnecessary death.

'He knew, you see. If I'd been long in the country, I wouldn't still be making silly mistakes with the money . . . I tried to say I'd always lived here, but he shook his head. He started saying, "You do realize what rabies can do to people, how they die from it?" I was carrying my hat. I'd arrived, you know, rather overdressed for the fête, and I'd taken it off. It was *you* told me that new people often bought a hat from Franchita, and I'd gone off and bought one. A very staid, old-fashioned one, which I thought would be right for Hexton. It had a pin. I had my fingers on the pin as he spoke.'

'And you had, of course, the necessary medical knowledge,' I said, my voice harsh, as I tried to put the picture from my mind: the pin sliding into the vital area, Marcus falling . . .

'Yes. I had the knowledge. I don't think it was a matter of thought, of considering whether, of deciding. I just pulled the pin out of the hat, and stuck it into him. Between the ribs, into the heart. Then I pulled it out, and pushed him over the side, as he was dying . . . I'm not going to apologize, or ask forgiveness . . . I can hardly recognize that it was me who did that . . . I was in some sort of trance, it came over me like a white heat, though I seemed perfectly cool on the surface. I walked on, then back home through town. I talked to people I knew, said what a successful fête it had been. Then I got back here, and I buried the pin in the garden, and then . . . Well, I can't tell you what I felt then. The sense of shame and self-disgust . . . mingled with a sort of exhilaration. It disgusts me now. I hate myself now—and yet, when I thought I was going to get away with it, I was almost . . . congratulating myself.'

She was stroking, obsessively, Gustaf's head.

'Well,' she asked in a low voice, 'what do we do now?'

'I don't know. I'm not sure that we do anything. I should tell you that, apart from what you've just told me, which nobody has overheard, the police have no evidence whatsoever that you killed Marcus. Nobody saw you do it, nobody even saw him coming after you along Castle Walk. There is the pin, of course: they might be able to do something if they found the pin. But at the moment, there is no case.'

'You don't understand,' she said, putting Gustaf gently down on the sofa. 'Perhaps they couldn't prove that I killed Marcus. But they could very easily prove that I have only been in this country three months or so, and that I brought Gustaf in illegally. And they will kill him, of course. There is no longer any point . . . I could kill him myself, rather than waiting for them to do it. I have plenty of stuff upstairs. But I don't think I could bring myself to do that. I could kill myself—much more easily I could kill myself—but it seems more fitting to . . . expiate—is that the word?—what

I did, in some way. Helen, did you say there were policemen outside?'

'Yes. One at the back, one at the front.'

'It wasn't necessary, you know. But how could you know? Will you do one thing for me? Will you take charge of Gustaf? Will you—will Marcus's partner—make sure that . . . what has to be done . . . is done quickly, in the humanest possible way? Perhaps you could be with him for the first injection? He knows you.'

She went to the door, without another glance at me or her dog. I heard her open the front door, and say to the policeman there:

'I wonder if you would be so good as to come with me to the police station?'

I took Gustaf in my arms, and from the front garden we saw them walking down the road towards town. Gwen Nilsson seemed to be carrying on a polite conversation, in the quiet, cool and efficient manner that I had liked from the first.

CHAPTER 18

AFTERWARDS

Ironically enough, they did not put Gustaf down. They don't always, though Gwen Nilsson didn't realize that. He was put into quarantine kennels for the remainder of his six months, then let out into the care of one of her neighbours, until such a time as she should be released from jail.

Which should not be long now. As with the lady recently who ran over her lover several times, and was released by the judge on the grounds that it was done at her difficult time of the month, so in this case the judge (who arrived at the Court each day in his limousine, with his two poodles on the back seat) was positively complimentary: this was an act—a foolish, wicked act—that was done on the spur of the moment by a thoroughly upright and responsible person; it was the sort of murder that was unlikely to happen again, springing as it did from a most unlikely combination of circumstances; what was more—here the judge became benevolently circumlocutory—the lady in question was going through The Change. Society would not be served, he thought, by a long sentence, so he gave her a very short one. 'It's a wonder he didn't let her off with a £10 fine,' I said bitterly afterwards.

But really I found it very difficult to sort out my emotions. I've never been one of the 'punish 'em until it hurts' brigade. But how could he be so sure that she would not do it again? How could he be sure that other people might not use his leniency as a precedent and an encouragement? Above all, I suppose, I asked: 'Was Marcus's life only worth two years?' Her house is sold, and soon she will be out. She will collect Gustaf, and go and live elsewhere. No doubt she will be discreet about her past. She's had experience in that.

And yet there is another part of me that says something else. When Superintendent Coulton came the day afterwards to talk it over, before he went back to Leeds, he said:

'I have to hand it to you. I'd never have thought of that motive. They say there aren't any new ones, but that *is* a motive I've never come across.'

'Nonsense,' I said. 'The motive was love. She murdered for love.'

And that, I suppose, was it. That was the reason why, in my less bitter moments, I didn't think so harshly of the judge.

Meanwhile Hexton goes on pretty much as before. Mary Morse has not been put away, but people have definitely realized that she's 'gone a bit funny', in local phrase. She smiles at people royally as she walks down the High Street, she delivers moral pronouncements à propos of nothing to innocent bystanders, she writes letters of instruction to the local mayor. One would not be surprised, if her house had a balcony, to see her doing '*Urbis et orbe*' from it to imagined crowds of pilgrims. Her God bus never, so to speak, got off the ground. She now takes a taxi, alone, to Shipford for Sunday service. Hawkins, the local taxi-man, then ferries a Shipford high churchman back for the Hexton service, so the score is 1-1. Hawkins himself is a Methodist and attends chapel in the evening, so he serves both God and Mammon, though not in that order.

Father Battersby's services settled down to attracting about fifteen or twenty more people than Walter Primp's, and this is thought of as a great triumph. Franchita goes regularly to them, because they seem to satisfy some of her inner hunger for drama. Otherwise she is slightly less bossy than before, but still makes regular visits to her dentist in Barnard's Castle. Howard Culpepper, I am quite sure, is fully aware of the purpose of these visits, but views them in the light of liberation for himself. Timothy Horsforth has moved away, to a flat in Darlington, and never returns, even for visits. I am occasionally allowed fill-in weeks of teaching at his father's school, but I like the man none the more. Rumours are beginning to get around about Fiona Weston ... Visitors to Harrogate report that Thyrza Primp is almost permanently installed at the windows of Betty's Tea Rooms, glaring at the tourists, and making a Yorkshire teacake go a very long way indeed.

I never did escape from Hexton, you notice. Perhaps I felt some shame at having blamed it for the murder of Marcus. I was wrong, after all: a woman living in Hexton did kill him, but not Hexton, not the spirit of the place. And then, the Battersby affair had taught me that there was another Hexton, which was not all tea-drinking and gossip and social churchgoing and 'nice' library books. This was a Hexton where it was perfectly possible to feel at home and be myself—not a particularly pleasant or comfortable thing to be, but it is the only self I have got.

There is one more reason why I have not left Hexton: a little over a year after Marcus's death, I married Father Battersby. But that is another and quite a different sort of story.

Robert Barnard has been nominated three times for mystery writing's highest honor, the Edgar Award. His most recent books include DEATH AND THE PRINCESS, CORPSE IN A GILDED CAGE, and OUT OF THE BLACKOUT. For seven years he was Professor of English Literature at the University of Tromsø in Norway, the northernmost university in the world. He and his wife, Louise, now live in Leeds, England.